CROSSDRESSING

CROSSDRESSING

EROTIC SHORT STORIES

EDITED BY
RACHEL KRAMER BUSSEL

FOREWORD BY
VERONICA VERA

CLEIS
PRESS

Published in the United States by Cleis Press Inc.,
P.O. Box 14697, San Francisco, California 94114.

Printed in the United States.
Cover design: Scott Idleman
Cover photo: Kevin Mackintosh
Text design: Frank Wiedemann
Cleis Press logo art: Juana Alicia
First Edition.
10 9 8 7 6 5 4 3 2 1

"Tori's Secret" by Andrea Miller was originally published in *Best Lesbian Erotica 2006*, edited by Tristan Taormino (Cleis, 2005). "Michelle, Ma Belle" by Marcy Sheiner was originally published in the newsletter *Private Lives*.

Contents

| FOREWORD

S ome years ago, before the birth of my crossdressing academy, I was invited to a costume party. I was dating a cop from Canada and he'd given me the shirt off his back, so I decided to go as a police officer. I found a pair of navy-blue trousers and wore black leather boots, but I still felt like a lady. It wasn't until I put on a tie that things changed. That skimpy, phallic fabric dangling from my neck caused a physical sensation. I no longer had firm breasts but a broad chest that swelled with authority. I stood taller, I felt stronger. As if by magic, I, the queen of femininity, felt like a man. And people's response to me was different, too. They gave me more space; they were more reticent and submissive. Before the night was over that visiting policeman felt my long arm of the law in places that certain states still called illegal.

That experience impressed me with the erotic power of crossdressing and to this day remains vivid. Since then, as the dean of Miss Vera's Finishing School for Boys Who Want to Be Girls, I've seen many times over how a tight corset can free the most shy from the confines of their inhibitions, or a lace nightie turn one who is well-armored into a delicious morsel of vulnerability. When invited by Rachel Kramer Bussel to write the foreword to this book, I was tickled pink. Too often, the art of crossdressing is presented in limited form, stripped of its sexual potential—but potential and limitless options are what crossdressing is really all about. The media will focus on the visual make-over—everyone likes to see the "before and after"—as long as the action stays on the surface and doesn't penetrate. How many times have I answered questions about the sexual orientation of my students as "the line between who is gay, straight, bisexual is a very blurry line, especially when you dress up and play with gender"? The eroticism of crossdressing is a subject that needs to be freed from the closet.

Leave it to Rachel, the Lusty Lady herself, to open this door. Rachel champions life with an erotic edge, and she also believes in the power of good writing. The combination is provocative, even subversive, just like crossdressing. In Elizabethan times, "sumptuary laws" were written to keep the masses in check. A man could not wear women's clothes, nor could a woman wear a man's. No one could wear clothing above his or her station, for fear that dressing too fine would give a person fancy ideas. A mingling of the classes could change the face and the figure of society, even lead to revolution. These laws were short-lived because they were impossible to enforce. When it comes to our imaginations and libidos, we humans are just too messy and chaotic. Reader beware, because the stories in this book can shake your status quo, excite you in ways you might not have thought possible, shred your resolve to ribbons. We all have invested our clothes with intangible qualities and they can take possession of us.

Here you will find literary temptations, guidelines for crossing erotic borders, with clothing and props that expose even as they camouflage. What you will not find in these stories are long inventories of outfits with no payoffs. When these characters pack, their purpose is not just to fill up a suitcase.

There are those who may deem this book politically incorrect (to me that's part of its charm). They prefer to keep sex and gender as two separate categories where never the twain shall meet. It is an attempt to make kink more conservative, and transgender more acceptable and less threatening, not only to outsiders but to those who themselves identify as transgender. Some will say, "Crossdressing is not about a different sexual orientation but about a different gender identity." But these stories invite all of us to experience ourselves as transcending gender, in practice or as literary voyeurs. Each one of us has the physical capacity—enough holes, appendages, and extensions—to give and to experience pleasure from any other.

I've always believed in the intimacy of sex, whether the scenario involves those who know each other well or total strangers. Stories such as these that delve into the minds of the players, as well as describe their actions, outfits, and accoutrements, bring us closer together, help us to understand one another, and increase family values—our human family values. We connect with the forces of creation alive within each of us. And we evolve. While you are reading these stories, whether alone or with a lover, if you are inspired to masturbate, as well you might be, enjoy the pleasure of your orgasms and know that by your pleasure you make the world a more enchanting place.

For your homework, why not form a reading group and get together with some friends and explore these texts in depth? Just remember to dress for the occasion.

Veronica Vera
New York City
March 2007

INTRODUCTION: CROSSING BOUNDARIES AND BENDING GENDERS

C rossdressing spans such a wide range of possibilities, erotic and otherwise, that the only thing we can safely say brings the mélange of its practitioners under one umbrella is that they dress (sometimes or all the time) in the clothing of another gender. In an age when gender is becoming increasingly fluid, deconstructed, questioned, and sometimes abandoned, we can begin to see the idea and reality of crossdressing in a new light.

This book focuses on the erotic pleasures of crossdressing, while also touching on the life-changing, mind-melting, earthshifting experiences that can come from actively playing with one's gender. For some characters, crossdressing means transgressing, transforming, subverting the rules to enter another body in order to enter another world, literally or figuratively. Sometimes it gives them permission to go where they'd be unwanted otherwise. For other characters, playing with their attire lets their minds create the fantasy creature they've always longed to be. It means acting, homecoming, freedom. Sometimes, it's a fun, risqué adventure, a break from the ordinary, a chance to see what might happen if you slipped into a dress or suited up. Would you be the same person? Would you feel the same? Would you get turned on in the same way? These questions and more get tackled in *Crossdressing,* though the answers are as varied as we are.

When these characters don the clothes of another gender, or another gender role, they find not just their bodies but their minds altered in powerful ways. What was once forbidden is now acceptable—or maybe it's still taboo but even hotter because of it. When they literally step into someone else's shoes, their bodies, minds, and libidos can explore passions they might not dare voice otherwise. Whether it's the bra, panties, and garter tucked away under the charcoal-gray business suit or the bound breasts flattened under a drag king's snazzy attire, clothes, as more than one character here can attest, do "make the man"—or woman—though the person inside those clothes creates his or her power from within as well.

In Stephen Albrow's "More Than Meets the Eye," his businessman protagonist has a secret under his suit that's his private treasure, until he chooses to share it: "My Brooks Brothers shirt is thick enough to cover up my white satin bra and garter belt, but not so thick that I can't feel the garter belt's lace trim as I run my fingertip over my abs. Just knowing this little bit of Suzy is there is enough to calm my nerves." Part of his narrator's delight is in fooling those around him. Yet revealing Suzy to her special lover is a bold thrill that yields untold rewards, and it's this push-pull of discovery and secrecy, of flaunting and hiding, of male and female that makes the story come alive.

These stories are not just about crossing genders but about living with the duality of one within the other, mixed together, mingling—the experience of living as one changing how a person lives as the other. Ashley Laine, the sensual, seductive drag queen narrator of Tulsa Brown's exquisitely rendered "Temporary," reveals the fear that haunts her at being found out: "When his thick fingers began to creep under my panties, I edged away, afraid to ripple the surface of his fantasy." Yet she proceeds, risking rejection for the joy of bringing that duality together into her erotic life. You can feel the shivers Rory delivers to her with the words "Oh, girl"—two simple but powerful words that encapsulate the crux of both Brown's story and this collection as a whole. When these characters—men, women, and those in between or neither at all—are finally able to be recognized for their chosen selves, the thrill goes far beyond the sexual.

Yet sex, desire, lust, and longing are front and center throughout, even as more complex gender dynamics come into play. In Debra Hyde's "Just Like a Boy," we learn that simply turning oneself into a "boy" is not enough for her narrator. She longs to be the boy of her childhood dreams, not "an androgyne in boy's clothes." Yet her venture into male territory isn't only for her but for her lover, Matthias, as well. Hyde draws out the tension in this dominant/submissive relationship, where power gets exerted in twisted, yet intriguing, ways.

The power of uniform gets invoked in Lisabet Sarai's humorous "Beefeater," in which a young British woman mocks family—and tradition—to dress in the garb of the Yeoman Warders guarding the Tower of London. The secrecy of her mission, combined with the defiant naughtiness of their endeavor, had me rooting for them with all the fervor of anyone who's deliberately disobeyed, half-hoping to get punished.

Crossdressers themselves aren't the only ones here with a tale to tell. In T. Hitman's "Higher and Higher," Pete pretends to be his naughty alter ego, Nate, when he hires Roni, a "dudette" who shows Pete a few tricks as she turns one, worshipping him in ways nobody else ever has. His internal dilemma, caught between sheer arousal and propriety, between who he thinks he should desire and who he actually does, gives us a peek into how those who lust after crossdressers of any variety also struggle to embrace their wants.

In *Crossdressing*, you'll find men in panties, butches in dresses, girls looking like boys, drag queens, drag kings, and those who can't be tidily summed up by their outer appearance. You'll find men who want to be men, only prettier, and women who don't have penis envy per se, but don't always want to be the little lady. In short, you'll find people across the sexual-orientation spectrum fucking with gender and gender roles—and simply fucking.

At one point, looking at herself in the mirror, Brown's drag queen says, "Some people might call this a fantasy, but it was my deepest truth." Here you get hot fantasy, fiction, and the kind of truth that really matters, the kind that gets under our skin, under our clothes, under our disguises to a place that speaks to us deep in our erotic souls. Whatever you're wearing right now (or not), I hope you'll join me on this tour across stages real and imagined, where the limits of gender-bending are in the eyes of the beholder.

Rachel Kramer Bussel
New York City
April 2007

TEMPORARY

Tulsa Brown

Listen," I said, "I'm going to take these heels off."

The dishwasher looked up. He was short and broad, dark as French roast coffee, muscles hard as an iron gate.

"I don't give a shit, man."

He laid a hair's emphasis on the last word, maybe to let me know he wasn't fooled by my red satin dress and the oak-brown hair that swept past my shoulders. Yet I distinctly remembered him looking when I'd waltzed from the dressing room to the club's little stage a few hours ago. His head turned so hard his vertebrae crackled.

And he was still staring. I slipped off one pump, then the other, dropping five inches to the kitchen's cool floor. The man was taller than me now, and I felt the vertigo thrall of fear and excitement. I loved to be looked at but I couldn't read his steady, nailhead eyes. I'd guessed wrong before. Terribly wrong.

I set the black patent shoes on top of the stainless-steel counter, spiked heels lined up, weapons if I needed them. It was 3 a.m. and we were the only ones left in the place. The dishwasher snorted and turned back to his work. I braced myself for my own—scraping and sorting. It was hard to imagine that a few hours ago people had been whistling for me, hooting and stomping on the floor, and now I was scraping their half-chewed food into the garbage. My stomach roiled. *Show business*, I thought with a grimace.

"How come you're doing dishes if you're a star?"

The words jarred me. The man's lip lifted on the edge of a sneer.

"Well, it was a charity event. Everybody pitches in. The others waited on tables and took tickets."

"But you got this."

Laughter lurked under the words. My hand went to my hip.

"Yes, I did. And guess what, Einstein: Tonight I'm going home and I'll never have to see this shithole again. I bet that you do—every single day."

His nostrils flared. "It's just temporary."

"So was income tax!"

For an instant we glared at each other. Then he seized an arm-breaking tray of dishes and hoisted it over to the sink, biceps straining his kitchen whites. I turned with an abrupt flounce, breasts swaying. I'd been performing with four others over the last six months, doing drag shows for charity benefits and the occasional gay bar gala. We usually worked for tips, but on bad gigs—like this one—we had to "assist the staff," too.

"We're making our names," Carl our MC said, over and over.

"I already have a name," I'd snapped at him. "And if somebody doesn't write it on a check real soon, I'm dumping this trailer-park talent show."

"Trailer park!" Carl snarled. "I've done Vegas!"

"So I heard—on your knees."

I thought he'd smack me, but his eyes suddenly narrowed. "It's not a bitch contest, darling. There is no prize."

That's when I started getting the crap jobs, yet he didn't dare cut me loose. I was a singer, a torch. The others only lip-synched, but I really sang, steel-note cries of longing that pierced the smoky haze. Up on the stage, blazing like a satin flame, I could hold the entire room in my palm—the men's desire, the women's envy. And in that instant my feet didn't hurt, and the four hours of shaving and waxing didn't matter. The bit of flesh strapped down tight between my legs no longer existed. I was Ashley Laine, a woman flying, not falling.

I won in other ways, too. When Carl walked out into the crowd, to fluff up interest and stroke a man or two, everyone laughed. That's because he looked like what he was—a hefty TV squeezed into his aunt's castoffs. He was six foot two in flats and wore a thrift-shop Doris Day wig. Pure plastic.

I was different. I strolled into the audience like a long-legged sylph, and the air sizzled. Tonight I'd put my foot on a big man's chair, between his legs, the patent leather toe just millimeters from his bulge. He was a burly trucker type, the kind who swore he'd never come to a place like this. In the dazzling glare of the spotlight, I let the red satin slide to the top of my thigh. I could hear his excited, quickening breath, feel his eyes scour my body—nipples, naked leg, my succulent painted lips. He was enthralled. I drank Carl's envy from across the room.

There is a prize, darling, I thought.

A clatter of pots made me turn. The dishwasher was still at the sink, jaw set, big shoulders moving with the precision of anger. Frayed male pride. I was sorry for what I'd said.

"What's your name?" I called over the noise.

He didn't look up. "What the hell do you care?"

"Oh, don't tease me. I know I've been naughty."

The last word caught him by surprise and he glanced over, grinning in spite of himself. After a moment he pulled out of the water and started toward me, wiping his hands on a towel. Closer was better. His whole upper body swayed when he walked, a sailor's big-armed swagger that made me catch my breath. There were amethyst highlights in his sienna skin; his lips and big palms were startlingly pink. The part of me flattened by the spandex panties began to thicken.

"Tell me yours first," he said.

"It all depends. If you're not a cop or my mother, I'm Ashley Laine."

His smile broadened. "Rory Park." He thrust out his hand and enveloped mine, a dark nest enfolding a pale little bird.

I squeezed back. "It would seem there's a Park at the end of the Laine."

He laughed abruptly, surprised again, a flash of white and wet pink that gave me a flutter. Damn, this was looking good.

"So, if this career is only temporary, what are you on your way to?" I said.

"Oh." He pulled away. "There's lots of possibilities. I've got lots of prospects."

He began to wander through the narrow aisles, his back to me. There was something about his knotted shoulders and the way he trailed his fingers along the stainless-steel counter that made my chest tighten.

"Are you on parole, Rory?" I asked quietly.

He looked back at me, chin tilted up, not exactly a dare. "You got a dick under that dress?"

My heart leapt into a trot but I held his gaze. "The last time I looked."

Rory smiled ruefully. "Yeah, me too. Last time I looked."

Great, I thought. *Another Mr. Right-cum-felon.* Yet I felt a strange sense of relief. This was the kind of news I usually got late in a relationship. Way too late. I turned to my dirty trays again and dove into the task with brisk energy. Finish up. Go home. Wang off if you have to.

But Rory didn't go back to his sink. He settled across the counter from me, leaned forward on his arms in a hard-sculpted, masculine trapezoid. "Hey, you're really something, you know? If I saw you on the street, I never would have guessed. I'm not queer or nothing, but you're pretty hot."

I should have kept my mouth shut, but he'd jabbed at an old, tired wound.

"Guess again—I'm not gay, either."

"What?" He pulled back, then grinned. "Ah, you're shittin' me."

I straightened, flushing.

"Here's a telegram for your thick male brain: It isn't always about sex. It isn't about what you stick where and into who. I'm a female who happens to have a male body—for the moment. You understand temporary, don't you, Rory?" I flipped my long hair with a toss of my head. "I'm not in drag, I'm...in process."

His gaze dropped to my breasts, to the bullet-firm nipples pushing against the silky fabric.

"So those are yours?"

He reached out—he was going to squeeze me like cantaloupe. I smacked him away so hard my own hand sparkled with pain. His eyes widened, a dark flash of lust and anger, and my heart leapt. I thought he might grab me across the counter.

Bang! Bang! Someone pounded on the heavy metal kitchen door, the one that led to the alley.

"Richard! Are you in there?" a voice called.

Oh, God. The voice skewered me like an icicle. "Don't open it," I said.

Rory glanced at the door, then at me again, bewildered. "Richard, don't screw with me, bitch! Carl nailed you. I know you're in there."

I reeled with the nausea of betrayal. I'd made some mistakes in the past, and I'd been running from this one for months. And Carl knew it—that asshole!

"What the hell is going on, Ashley?" Rory hissed.

"Don't do anything. I'll check for another exit."

I hiked up my skirt and sprinted away, dodging around the club's tables. I reached the front door and yanked on it. Damn! It could only be opened with a key. By the time I was back in the kitchen, Rory's hands were on his hips, his broad chest puffed with anger.

My ex was kicking at the door now, a terrifying rattle. Thank God it only opened from the inside.

"The front's locked," I panted.

"Look—does he pack a gun?"

"Not...always."

"Shit!" Rory whammed the counter with the flat of his hand and the dishes jumped. Bad news. My ex renewed his assault on the door.

"I know you're in there, you lying slut!"

Rory shot me a hard look. This wasn't his fight or his problem.

"All right. I'm calling the cops," I blurted.

I was almost into the hallway when he seized my arm.

"No—please." His eyes were large, liquid, frightened. "My parole is in another state."

The revelation opened inside me. If the police showed up, Rory was the one going to jail. Yet he wasn't threatening me, he was asking. It was a strange sensation to have this big man pleading with me.

"But what am I going to do? If I walk out of here, I won't get home." I could hear the shrill, desperate note in my voice. "And if we don't get rid of him, someone else will call the cops."

Rory hesitated, then held a finger to his lips. Shh. He strode back to the metal door and wound up and hammered it with the side of his fist.

"What the hell are you wailing about, man?" he roared.

There was a second's stunned silence. My ex wasn't expecting that deep basso.

"I'm looking for a bitch named Richard. Someone told me he's in there."

"That nut in the dress? I sent him home an hour ago. The most useless piece of shit I ever had in my kitchen."

The pain was swift, a boot in the stomach. But Rory held up his hand to me—hold on.

"Well, just let me in to check," my ex said.

"I open this door and my balls are breakfast. Staff only."

"You've gotta come out sometime." The threat was dark, rumbling, a storm I already knew.

"Yeah, I do," Rory called. "But I hope you brought a chair, man. I'm night crew. I don't walk for another five hours."

Silence. I twisted on the hook, fingernails digging into my palms.

"Fuck." The word was a low thud of defeat, the last stone pitched backward by a man leaving. For long seconds Rory and I were transfixed, straining for more sounds, but there was nothing. At last I exhaled, a rush of relief that punctured me like a balloon. I backed against a wall and slid down, bones melting. I put my hand over my face, eyelashes trembling against my palm. Don't cry, don't cry.

Just another day at the office, I thought bitterly. Betrayed, threatened, terrified. And for what? So I could stand on a stage for three minutes and feel...real? All I wanted was someone who understood the woman I was going to be and yet desired me now, too. Instead, I found lovers who loathed themselves for wanting me. I felt like a wineglass—a toast you drank, then smashed in the fireplace.

"What was the name of that song you sang tonight?" Rory's voice was soft.

I looked up, blinking tears. He was back at the sink, washing quietly.

"'Skylark.' It's an old jazz tune."

He nodded without looking at me. "It was beautiful. Sad but beautiful. It pulled me right out of the kitchen. They wouldn't let me out front to watch, but I stood in the hallway, listening."

The surge of gratitude almost closed my throat. In that instant his few words meant more than the waves of applause that had rolled out to me under the spotlight. It kindled an idea that pulled me to my feet.

"Rory, why don't you take a break? Go sit down at a table, relax for a bit." He turned. I was leaning against the wall, head tilted back, my bare neck arching out toward him. At last a slow, smoky smile lit up his handsome face.

"All right."

I gave myself three minutes in the dressing room to brush my hair and freshen my makeup. On impulse, I peeled off my stockings, and the rich, smooth fabric of my dress caressed my bare thighs as I moved. Anticipation ran over me like waves of champagne. I stepped into my high heels again, and the sudden lift straightened me, thrust my silicone breasts forward. The dark-eyed siren in red who gazed back from the mirror was a flame. A torch. Some people might call this a fantasy, but it was my deepest truth.

Rory hadn't turned on the lights. The spillover glow from

the hall swept out over the empty tables in a soft, dreamy wash. He'd lit the candle on his table and sat upright in the chair, dark hands on his white, uniformed thighs. Anxious. Peeking from behind the partition, I took a breath to slow my pounding heart, then stepped out of the shadows and began to sing.

"Well, the men come in these places, and the men are all the same..."

The long night had rasped my voice to husky velvet, and I softened Tina Turner's "Private Dancer" to a lullaby. Each stride a slow undulation, my long, pale legs emerging through the slits of the skirt, then retreating. A tease. I let my elegant, gleaming nails skim the surface of the polished tables.

Rory's gaze was rapt, devouring. I meandered toward him, exhilarated by the desire I could feel radiating from his body. When he reached between his thighs and squeezed the bulge, longing leapt beneath my dress.

"I'm your private dancer, a dancer for money..."

I'd reached him at last and slid my ass onto his tabletop. The flickering candle lit up the sheen of sweat on his throat; his eyes had the glaze of a dream. I settled a foot against his thigh, the spiked heel indenting the muscle, and crossed one leg over the other, close enough that his warm, quick breath whispered over my naked knees. He closed his hand around my ankle, then leaned forward and opened his mouth on my bare calf in a soft, wet bite. Desire twisted the song in my throat to a moan.

He stood to embrace me, and I spread my knees wide to receive him, still perched on the table like an ornament. He opened my mouth with a demanding kiss, entered me with his tongue. I sucked on it eagerly, wanting to take him inside me any way I could. When his thick fingers began to creep under my panties, I edged away, afraid to ripple the surface of his fantasy. He pulled away from my lips and panted lightly against my ear.

"I want to see you—your hard-on and tits. I want to see it all."

I prickled with apprehension. I'd never done this for anyone, not in a dress. "Close your eyes first."

Rory took a step back, grinning faintly, and did as he was told. The hard jut in his white pants made my mouth swim. I slipped off my underwear, and my erection surged to full height, a slender rapier bobbing under the weight of the swollen bell cap. I gathered my skirt back and let it cascade down both sides in a satin waterfall. When I gently stroked myself, the tingling rush was amplified. Dizzying. The feminine fabric against my skin and the big-boned male in front of me were a potent cocktail.

"All right," I said.

Rory opened his eyes. For a second he just stared, eyes darting from my face to my breasts to the erection I still tugged between my legs.

"Oh, girl," he breathed. "You're so fine."

Oh, girl. The words ran through me in an electric current. I squeezed myself, my cockhead surging in a sweet throb on top of my delicate fist. Rory unzipped, clumsy with want, fumbled with his shirt and sent a button sailing. It rolled in a spiral on the ugly burgundy carpet. Then he gathered me up and swept me down to that carpet, too.

He was vast, dark, undulating—a powerful wave of a man. I was the red sunset dancing on his surface. On the club floor between the tables, I lapped at his chest and sucked hard on his nipples, feeling his low, hungry sounds vibrate against my lips. He touched me with a rough, working man's awe, as if he were afraid he might break something.

"It's my real hair," I said. "You can pull on it."

Emboldened, he wrapped the silky length around his fist, tight enough to make my scalp burn. But it wasn't pain—as soon as he stepped into a wide-legged stance in front of my mouth.

His cock was the color of an angry plum, a swaggering brute that twitched toward me, taut and urgent. I licked the underside of the fleshy ridge, teased the satin surface with my teeth. Rory growled in his throat and urged me forward, his fist at the base of my skull. When I opened my mouth to take his full length, he thrust forward and stretched me wide. It was like being entered—deep, thrilling, necessary.

I gripped both his thighs for better balance, and he pushed one of my hands away.

"No, work your dick. Ride it, baby. I want to see you come."

I didn't need a second invitation. I flipped up my skirt again, and we fell into an extraordinary rhythm, pumping like a machine with two pistons. He bucked into my mouth, and I rode my own familiar grip, stoked by sensation and the thick, guttural sounds of his pleasure. My own rushed up quickly, churned in my balls in exquisite curls. I gripped my cock around the base, stalling.

Rory was driving faster, harder. Every time he hit the back of my throat, the impact hurtled down through me and throbbed between my legs. He was fucking my whole body through my mouth. Just as I wondered how long I could hold off, he yanked my head back. His cock pulled out with a soft slurp, my mouth hung open in a surprised O.

"Come!" Rory blurted.

The jets struck my bare chest like hot cream, pulse after pulse that snaked down into my cleavage. The triumph released me—my own bliss caught me in that instant, a low thunder that pulled a cry from my center. I clung to his thigh and rode one galloping wave after another, spasms twisting me, wrenching me with joy as I shot far out between his legs.

The floor was hard and it didn't matter; we floated on a languid stream. I lay in the crook of his big arm and watched the faint flickering of the candle against the ceiling high above. A corner of my mind nagged at me: Rory's record, his broken parole. But I refused to worry about it tonight. Happiness was the most temporary thing of all.

"I guess I owe you a dress." Rory touched the stains below my neckline, which where were already starting to stiffen.

"The night's not over," I said. "It could be two."

He laughed, a single happy note that gave me courage. I rolled onto my side and nestled my cheek against his chest.

"What made you want me?" I asked softly. "Seeing that you're not queer."

Rory took a breath. "Oh. Because you're beautiful and you looked so alone.

"We're all...kind of alone, if you think about it." He hesitated shyly.

"Nobody ever sang for me before."

I heard the words yet felt something else beneath them, as delicious and intimate as a squeeze. *Oh, girl.*

I fluttered my fingernails down his chest in a teasing, butterfly trail.

"And she just might sing for you again."

JUST LIKE A BOY

Debra Hyde

The package arrived on Monday at 12:37 p.m., and I knew it was from Matthias by the Celtic knot it bore. All of Matthias's prized possessions bore that mark, that infinite loop of green and yellow. His car wore it via a decal, his laptop computer via its screen saver, and me via a tattoo. Male territorial marking, it was, and I had fallen in love with him because he was man enough to mark me.

If the sight of his mark tripped me up, then the contents of the box stopped me cold. As I pulled the flaps of the cardboard box open and looked inside, I knew what Matthias had sent me: permission to be a boy. He had packed everything a boy needed to be himself: baggie denim shorts, briefs (not boxers!), hefty boots and a T-shirt two sizes too big. To my dismay, the T-shirt didn't promote the testosterone statements of the Butthole Surfers or Limp Bizkit. Instead, it featured the silk-screened image of Boy, the tousled-hair urchin from the Johnny Weissmuller *Tarzan* movies.

Typical Matthias. To his thinking, all boys should lose themselves in the works of Edgar Rice Burroughs. I haven't yet had the heart to tell him that Burroughs's books have been out of print for years.

As I rummaged through the clothes, a second, much smaller box appeared. My pulse raced—I was thinking it might be the one thing I needed to properly transform myself. I tore into it, hoping to find a respectable seven inches waiting for me, but instead I found a gay-porn video with a Post-it note commanding me to "watch and learn."

A porn video but no dick? What was Matthias thinking?

But I watched and learned, as instructed. I watched a handsome young stud go down on an older, mature fuckbuddy. I watched how he eagerly took a massive amount of dick into his mouth, how he sucked and slurped its entire length, how he took it like a man when his lover wanted to let loose. I watched him lie down on his back, raise and spread his legs to get greased for more action. I watched him take dick up the ass in a battering ram of a fuck until his top pulled out and sprayed him with bullets of come.

So that's what Matthias wanted from me. His dick down my throat and a hearty ass fuck. Fair enough. But when I saw the kid grab his own cock and work his hand like a piston, my heart sank. When I witnessed him geyser with come, my mood deflated way faster than his big dick.

After all, what good was being a hot boy fuck if you didn't have a cock to call your own?

Two days after the first package arrived, a second parcel came in the mail and I finally had a dick to call my own. Unfortunately, it did nothing to end my disappointment from the previous days. Instead of hoisting a huge, man-size cock from the package, I fished out a skinny little four-incher, a prick so small that it was hardly worth the effort of packing it into my pants.

Except I knew that I'd catch holy hell from Matthias if he didn't find it in place the next time he grabbed me by the crotch. Not long ago, when I revealed my girlhood desires for boyhood to him, he had laughed, stuck his hand between my legs, and said, "So you want a basket to call your own, eh?" He had squeezed me as he spoke. Hearing queer words from a straight man's lips caught me by surprise, but then I remembered him saying how he once had cruised gay bars out of sheer sexual frustration and how "Kinsey" he was. He was a spectrum of a man.

Soon after making my quirky disclosure, Matthias took to teasing me about my latent boyness, telling me how much rougher gay sex was than straight sex. At least the way he wanted gay sex—with leather and whips and humiliating trials of manhood.

"I'll put a cigar out on your thigh, kid. Think you can take it?"

"Maybe I'll turn you over to some leathermen and watch them beat you."

"There's always the biker way of breaking a boy in—leather gloves and circle jerks."

Each time he teased me, his scenarios became more fantastic, more lurid, and more arousing. My cunt ached to be a hard dick when he talked like that. Which made me ache to pack a dick big enough to say that I could take it, maybe even dish it out, too. But is that what I got? No. I got a teeny fucking peeny.

Thanks a lot, Matthias.

Yeah, I was an ingrate and I've milked my bad mood for all it was worth. I've pouted. I've sulked. I've moped around the house. Just like a boy who hadn't gotten his way.

Just like a boy—just the boy in me, the boy that started his fight for attention the first time my mother tried to curl my hair and put me in a frilly dress. I was three years old, and pictures show me crying and mad and clutching my Easter present, a tall but soft plush bunny that sagged in my arms. Defiantly, I had named him Robert, telling my parents in no uncertain terms that "he isn't a girl." That morning, I wanted to be like Robert, like my brother, even like my bald-headed meanie of a father. I wanted to be anything but a girl.

Eventually, I outgrew Robert but I still waged my fights against curls and frills. My parents gave up on the holiday pictures and shifted the battleground to school pictures. Kindergarten: pixie haircut and an olive-green jumper (so Jacqueline Kennedy). First grade: curls, but at least the sweater was blue. Second grade: even more curls, red sweater. (I narrowly avoided pink.) And finally third grade, the ultimate humiliation. My mom permed my mousy hair and made me wear a clown-collared dress in a patchwork-quilt pattern. I begged her not to do that to me, but she set her jaw and kept her eyes on the curlers. But when she saw the pictures and realized that I *did* look like a clown, she gave up. After that, I smiled at the camera, hair straight as straw, in dresses plain as gunnysacks.

As a teen, I shucked the dresses for pants completely, thanks to a relaxed dress code at school and women's pantsuits everywhere making denim for girls acceptable. But even then I pushed the envelope. I tossed my makeup and my bra, and swiped some hand-me-down shirts from my younger brother. For my entire sophomore year in high school, I dressed grunge decades before grunge existed.

No one noticed. No one even raised an eyebrow. I guess that, in the days of glitter and glam, a crossdressing girl flew under everyone's radar. I even escaped detection as a senior when I filled out my yearbook profile and deemed "dresses" to be my personal pet peeve. Hopes dashed, I gave up. I decided gender-bending was for boys only and went off to college and left the boy behind.

But I couldn't really forget the boy. Now, many years later, he lives within me, immature and shy, hiding behind my middle-age self-confidence. Oh, he hasn't had to put up with jewelry or heels or girly dresses all these years, but he also hasn't been able to come out and play. He's unrealized.

And because of that, so am I.

Saturday finally arrived. All week long I fantasized about how I'd look as a boy. I eyed men's underwear ads in lifestyle magazines and wondered which guy I'd most look like. On the street, I spied on men's crotches the way men do with women's tits and wondered what kind of basket each body held. I imagined myself out in the world, moving with a swagger, gruff and determined. I pretended that a dick made all the difference in the world.

But as I looked into the mirror and started working the gel into my hair, all my bravado vanished. Instantly. Because as I spiked and sprayed my hair, the image that stared back at me wasn't that of a boy. It wasn't even the image of a woman passing as a boy. What stared back was ambiguous and totally unexpected.

A lump of anxiety and disappointment formed in my throat. What do I do with this, I wondered?

I went into my bedroom and stood before my full-length mirror, but it didn't change anything. There I stood, an androgyne in boy's clothes. I went into the "maybe" mode of worry—maybe I should've gotten some fake facial hair, like the drag kings use. Maybe I should've suggested a suit or a prep school uniform. Maybe I should risk punishment and stuff a sock in my pants. Maybe I should just forget the whole thing.

Then it hit me. Matthias liked this look because I couldn't

hide what I really was—a tomboy who had matured into an adult, into a person who was more comfortable with men's casual wear and rough sex than with cosmetics, fashion accessories, and home decorating.

Being in boy's clothing felt natural and looked natural, to me at least. Packing a dick, even a miniscule one, felt downright great. But they didn't make me a boy. And looking at myself in the mirror, I began to wonder what would.

The doorbell sounded and I met Matthias at the door, bringing my confusion with me. When he saw me, a "this is perfect" smile washed across his face. He was pleased with what he saw and he wasted no time in showing me. He grabbed me by the scruff of the neck and planted a rough kiss on me. He pried my teeth apart with his tongue and devoured me. His free hand went right for my crotch and grabbed what little he found there. He rubbed his hand up and down my little bulge.

I should've blushed at first touch, but before I could react, Matthias moaned with such lust that his response stunned me. He was getting off on the prick in my pants! I mean, I was prepared for being a faggot boy, but somehow I'd failed to realize that the man who loved cunt—my cunt—would be queer too by virtue of getting hard over my dick.

But hey, what worked for him worked for me, and I humped Matthias's hand with my boy cock as thoughts of a rampaging ass fuck raced in my head.

Matthias pulled away from me and laughed. "Forget that, kid," he said as he dragged me by the neck over my hall staircase. "Kneel," he ordered. As I did, he sat on the stairs, planting himself so his crotch was mouth-level to me.

"Take out my dick and get it in your mouth—pronto!"

I hustled over his belt, his pants' button, his zipper, and freed his half-hard meat from his pants. I put my lips around his cock, just below its crown. At first touch, it swelled, big and hard, and stretched my lips tight.

"Suck me off," Matthias commanded.

Like he needed to tell me with words.

I went to work, trying to take him deep, just like in the video. I wanted to get as much of his dick down my throat as possible. I wanted to know how it felt, man-wise. But every time I got a mouthful of cock, I gagged and sputtered and drooled.

"Need a little help, boy?"

A rhetorical question. Matthias took over the action and face-fucked me, pushing his cock into me, pulling back against the roof of my mouth, setting a grueling, punishing pace. My reactions didn't change—I still gagged and sputtered—but Matthias controlled me with his cock and turned me into a hole. He fucked my face with such a ruthless focus that I wondered if he'd come that way.

He wouldn't. Instead, he grabbed me by the hair and pulled me back to the head of his cock. He directed me to suck there, just at the head of his cock. Puppet-like, I performed to perfection, and that little bit of mouth bobbing up and down on his dick put him just where he wanted to be. Grunting, Matthias came in a series of long, satisfying spasms.

Come shot into the back of my throat, hot and plentiful and with such force that it threatened to gag me one last time. Somehow, I managed not to choke. Somehow, I managed to savor every swallow.

"Yeah, that's it," Matthias congratulated me as he pulled his dick from my mouth, as I licked my lips. "That's it," he repeated as he patted my head, as I glowed with his approval. As he squirreled away his cock, he said, "Come on, we're got some men to go see."

Men to go see. So this was it; this was the moment of truth.

Maybe I should've worried right then about it, but I didn't. I was too busy glowing from my immediate success, from Matthias calling me kid and boy, treating me like a man and making me give good head. Yes, the moment of truth might very well lie ahead, and I might very well flunk. But for now, I basked in the moment at hand, a moment of satisfaction—a moment in which I felt just like a boy.

What more could I ask for?

HALLOWEEN

Helen Boyd

W hy don't you go in drag?" she asked him. She'd seen the fascination he had with her lingerie and how he was so careful when he picked stuff out for her. He had delicious taste: Brazilian-cut panties and delicate laced underwire bras in matching sets. Gorgeous. She was surprised to find herself titillated by the idea of putting him in the beautiful things he had bought her.

"I don't think I'll look very good," he answered, but as soon as she realized he *didn't* say, "That's sick," she knew she had a chance.

Halloween came around, and he hadn't thought of another costume, and they had to go to a party they'd been invited to: The hosts were people who could get her a lot of work. Because it was a fashion-industry crowd, she knew he couldn't do the usual straight-guy "mask and jeans" boring thing, so she spent the day picking out items of hers she thought would fit him. When he came home, she took all his clothes off and taught him how to shave his legs.

He was really surprised; his legs felt as smooth as hers when she was done, and he couldn't stop touching them. When she got on her knees to put the pair of nylons on, he was surprised he was hard—but he convinced himself that was because she was on her knees, which put him in the mood for a blow job.

She knew it was the delicious feel of the nylon on his newly shaved legs that had gotten him hard, but she wasn't about to fill him in for fear he'd back out.

It wasn't easy to get his cock into a pair of her panties—they weren't built for that—but she found a pair that worked well enough, and because they were snug, they even made his cock less visible. She put him in a padded bra stuffed with old shoulder pads of hers, and then a fitted blouse, a snug, knee-length pencil skirt, and a regular pair of black pumps she'd found at Payless. She wasn't about to buy him better shoes than her own! Besides, his shoes needed to be sturdy, because he was now going as Joan Crawford, as that's how he'd turned out.

She herself went as the "It girl," the silent girly film star who wore snug dresses and looked as innocent as her body didn't. Together they were a stunning pair of Weimar-era lipstick lesbians.

The first time she kissed him on the way out she was surprised by the feel of kissing lipsticked lips and the bump his "breasts" gave her own! She was way more turned on by this than she'd expected, and so was he. Every straight man has a thing for lesbians, but it had never occurred to either of them that they could be lesbians themselves, at least for a night.

Everyone at the party had fabulous costumes—some of them home creations, some obviously costing a fortune. There were a Marie Antoinette and Louis XV, a single and sultry Morticia

Addams (looking for her Gomez, she assumed), a car wreck of four people full of gore with bits of broken glass glued to their clothes, and, of course, one guy in Droogie's clothes, a *Clockwork Orange* punk.

Her boyfriend was the only boy in drag, as far as she could tell, and everyone loved how he looked. They didn't even know it was her boyfriend at first but thought she'd brought a girlfriend (not in costume), instead. She loved that. When people looked close—and when he talked—they knew it was him. But if he hadn't said a word, no one would have known.

Watching him carefully sit down so as not to expose himself tickled her. A guy dressed as Lawrence of Arabia asked him if he wanted a drink, and the look on both of their faces when he said yes in his baritone made her laugh so hard. "Lawrence" was not one to show that he was shocked, so got the "lady" a drink anyway. Her boyfriend's embarrassment had even made him a little coy when he accepted it, and that suited his costume even better.

One couple in particular intrigued her: They'd come as James Dean and Sal Mineo, so in a sense they were crossdressed as well—but as men. The whole joke of their costume was that they had made the unspoken sexual relationship between the rebel and his friend more obvious. They kissed and grabbed each other's packages in a way that was both playful and very sexual. Laura found herself wondering what the girl (Sal Mineo) looked like as a girl, and couldn't really tell. She looked back at her boyfriend sitting on the couch with his—she laughed when she saw it—legs crossed, and realized no one could really tell what he really looked like, either.

She leaned over the couch to point the couple out to her boyfriend, who was scanning some comic books the hosts had left on their coffee table, probably precisely for people like him. She felt eyes on her ass as soon as she did it, but instead of getting up quickly to see who was looking at her so intently, she talked to her boyfriend a little longer than she had planned, enjoying the stranger's eyes on her curvaceous body. Her boyfriend was so nervous and distracted by his own costume he hadn't really noticed how sexy she looked in hers, and suddenly Laura realized what a charge it was to feel a man's eyes on her like that. Having willingly turned her own boyfriend into a woman for the night, she now realized she already missed being looked at by a man.

By the time she stood up and subtly looked around, whoever had been looking at her had stopped.

Her boyfriend didn't dance because generally he didn't and he wasn't going to try in heels. The shoes were killing him, anyway, which is why he'd settled on the couch. Every time she brought him a drink or leaned over to tell him something, she felt the eyes again, and about the sixth time she looked up fast enough to see that it wasn't one set of eyes but two that were scoping her lovely booty. Both Sal and James, the homosexual couple, were checking her out. She found that pretty amusing—that a couple who were going as homosexuals were in fact probably one heterosexual and one bisexual...why else would Sal be looking at her ass, too?

In the meantime, she had met a few people who could get her work, and she was as charming and sexy as she could be, leaning forward to show off her décolletage as often as possible. She had at least five business cards in her vintage purse by 1 a.m. and decided to work a little less and have a little more fun.

By about 2 a.m., she was standing in the kitchen smoking near the window, when James Dean came in. She could tell he was normally a handsome man, but he had put on enough costume-type makeup to look a little like the real James Dean. He also had a charge to him, like the real James Dean, something a little menacing. He pulled at his black leather driver's gloves a little too often, she thought.

She was intrigued and, despite herself and her love for her boyfriend, she leaned a little out the window to see if she would feel his eyes on her again. She did. It was fail-safe. She started to feel like she was going to spend the whole evening bending over just to feel that stare. It turned her on very much, as did the old-fashioned lingerie she was wearing beneath her light-blue satin skirt. Shoot, even the satin turned her on, and the corset—despite keeping her from eating very much—made her stand up straighter. The sight of her own cleavage was surprisingly sexy. Though she'd never had much up top, the corset certainly made the most of it.

James Dean had to move a little closer to her when a very large Marie Antoinette—complete with panniers—had to get to the refrigerator. She felt herself go a little short of breath and tried to convince herself it was the corset or the cigarette, but she knew it was the proximity of that leather-clad hand. She wanted desperately to lean into it, just to feel it on her ass—when someone stepped on Marie's hem in the tight little kitchen, which sent the whole group bumping into one another like a chain of dominos. She felt like she'd made it happen by wishing so hard—then she felt James Dean's leather-clad hand on her ass, and the other grabbed her corseted waist. They were face to face, and no one, at that proximity, could fail to notice the rise and fall of her breasts. Somehow the corset made her breathing more extreme, and while she noticed him looking at her, he watched her breathing and lifted his eyes.

She had never felt such a charge.

As if on cue, or motivated by that weird sixth sense women

just have, Sal Mineo walked in. She was obviously put off by finding her boyfriend so tête-à-tête with another woman—and a curvaceous one at that. She had no curves of her own that night, having hidden them to be Sal Mineo. For a second, she felt like the object of her desire, and jealousy, was Laura and not James. She was playing the guy, after all, and felt a kind of masculine cockiness overtake her. She wanted to protect her girl from this interloper, and had to remind herself that the interloper was her actual boyfriend, not some stranger, and she didn't know this woman she was feeling so protective of at all.

Everyone had had a little too much to drink and the costumes were messing with everyone's heads—and libidos.

James took his hands off Laura, and Sal walked up and introduced himself. "I'm James's girlfriend," she said proprietarily, and then, surprising herself, added, "What a great corset." James took off and Laura and Sally—her real name—talked about corsets for a while. Sally had worn one to be an oversexed Little Bo Peep one year and had found it as sexy as Laura did tonight.

Sally asked if she was with anyone, and Laura pointed out her boyfriend, still primly sitting with his skirt tucked in under his legs.

Before either of them knew it, they were telling each other stories as if they were old friends. Sally had dated a crossdresser before she met James, and she had been very turned on by the whole thing, much more so than she had expected. Unfortunately, he'd been immature and commitment-phobic, so now she was with James, whom she had never gotten into drag but would have loved to—and thought secretly he'd love it, too. Laura confided that she was surprised how much it turned her on to see her boyfriend in drag, how smooth his legs were after she'd shaved them, how sexy even the shaving had been. "It's never that sexy when I shave my own," Laura laughed, and Sally agreed. She had shaved her ex's legs once, too.

By about 3, James and Laura's boyfriend were watching some late-night noir movie that seemed to be more about cleavage than killing, and Laura and Sally had shared their sexual histories. They had also discovered that they all lived in Brooklyn, and the two girls had decided it'd be best to share a cab.

On the couch, both men were half watching the movie and kind of talking to each other. "I'm a guy, I'm straight, it's just a costume," Laura's boyfriend had explained when James had seemed cautious about sitting down next to him. "I thought maybe you were..." James started to say "gay," and Laura's boyfriend shook his head and pointed behind him toward the kitchen, at Laura, and James understood that meant she was his girlfriend, so James sat down. Since then they'd just been two guys, except that every once in a while James turned and noticed how long and gorgeous Laura's boyfriend's legs were.

"Don't those shoes hurt?" James asked.

"Like a bitch," he answered. "That's why I'm sitting." James looked at his feet and legs again, as if he couldn't not look. "You've got better legs than most women," he said, surprised that he found them kind of attractive. "If I didn't know you were a guy and if I didn't have a girlfriend..." and then he laughed, embarrassed. "But you are a guy and I do have a girlfriend. You need a beer?"

Laura's boyfriend said yes, and James got up to get them two. He smacked Sally's ass as he walked by her on the way to the refrigerator. Laura felt a tiny shiver go through her; he was still wearing those gloves, and he smacked her in such a way as if to announce he owned that ass. Her boyfriend never did anything like that, and Laura wondered if she hadn't decided to dress him as a girl because he *was* sort of a girl. He certainly

didn't do supermasculine sexy things like that to her, ever. She
sighed. She was jealous, and torn. She and Sally were getting on
like sisters, and she felt guilty that she found her new friend's
boyfriend attractive.

James brought Laura's boyfriend the beer, and his press-on
nails accidentally brushed the tiny oval of skin on the back of
James's hand. James liked long nails.

"He's a little too macho," Sally told Laura after James left,
"but he's got a big dick." Laura smiled a little sickly: She'd
been smoking and drinking too much. Because of the corset, she
hadn't eaten a lot, either. She really hadn't needed to know that
those leather-clad hands led to a big dick.

Sally saw the look on Laura's face and apologized. "Too
much information—sorry." Laura just smiled sickly again.
"You think we should go? I hate to be the last ones to leave."

They looked around, and although there was no fear of them
being last, the party had thinned out pretty significantly, and
they weren't close friends of the hosts, either. Sally agreed, and
playing the man because she was dressed as one, let Laura walk
ahead of her. She couldn't help but think that was one heck of
a corset and one heck of a skirt, but that if Laura hadn't had
such a curvaceous body, neither would have looked as good as
they did.

They found a cab, and obviously it was James who had to sit
in the front. Once they were all in, shoes, handbags, and all, he
made a joke to the cabbie about taking his three whores home
with him. "That is *not* funny," Sally said and smacked him in
the back of the head. "Anyway, I'd be a hustler dressed like this,
not a whore." They all laughed. She was one cute little pretty-
boy, just as Sal Mineo had been.

They were so busy laughing and talking the whole way that

James had only gotten out his and Sally's address. When they arrived there, the cabbie said he wasn't going on to another stop, that he had to be told that beforehand. Both of the guys cursed him out ("First time he's ever been cursed out by Joan Crawford," Sally said to Laura as they watched the guys get on their macho), but Sally suggested they come up and have a nightcap before calling a car service to get home. They did.

Sally got drinks and James put on some music, and Laura and "Joan" kissed in the entrance. "There are lesbians getting it on in our living room," Sally yelled to James, and he came running. "Well, I guess they are lesbians, aren't they?" He stood and watched a little hungrily, a little drunk.

"Sorry, Laura, but your boyfriend has some fantastic legs." She was wearing a long skirt and hitched it up to show hers off. James was obviously impressed. "Not bad. Now if you two keep getting it on, I'll have plenty to think about when Sally goes to Dallas on business next week." Sally called him a pig and threw a cork at him from the kitchenette.

"All you straight boys and your lesbian fetish," she yelled. "Those girls in the movies aren't real lesbians, you know."

"I don't care about real lesbians," James concluded, but Laura's boyfriend had backed off a, feeling a little weird at being seen as a woman. He didn't have an issue with being seen as a lesbian, of course—that was sexy to him, too. "God, you're so dumb," Sally continued. "That's not even two girls and you're turned on watching them kiss. What an idiot. If I kissed her dressed like this you'd see a straight couple, when really we'd be lesbians! Duh."

A really weird silence enveloped the room. James broke it. "Well, let me see, and I'll tell you if I can tell." Laura's boyfriend—not macho like James—was secretly hoping they'd take James up on the dare. Sally was feeling a little manly herself in tight jeans packing a rolled-up sock, and walked up to Laura confidently, put one hand on the small of her back and the other in her hair and kissed her theatrically but deeply.

"More please," Laura's boyfriend said quietly.

"What did you say?" Laura asked, totally surprised, once Sally had stopped kissing her. They all looked at Laura's boyfriend.

"I said 'more please.' " This time it was Laura who rose to the challenge, and she grabbed Sally the same way she'd grabbed her and kissed her, theatrically again, but that kiss lasted a little longer. Laura was feeling very playful and very turned on. "This turn you on, Robert?" she asked. She kissed Sally again.

Sally laughed. "You didn't know about men and their lesbian fetish?" She kissed Laura and began unbuttoning her own shirt. "Watch this," she said both to the boys and to Laura as she pulled her shirt off. She was wearing no bra and had small A-cup breasts. She kissed Laura again.

"God, this is perfect," James said. "One blonde, one brunette. One with huge tits and one with little ones. Life is good." Laura's boyfriend agreed.

Laura and Sally were getting completely carried away, not taking any of it too seriously, but things were getting a little crazy. Sally had already done a striptease, unbuttoning her jeans like a pro. She let the sock fall, and stood in nothing but a pair of white boy-cut panties. She was the classic tomboy: small-breasted but blond, pretty but athletic. And Laura, of course, felt like the girliest of girls now, with her heaving cleavage and high heels.

Sally jokingly grabbed Laura's ass the next time she kissed her. It was all so dumb and theatrical, but the boys on the couch were getting turned on by it, which made the girls laugh harder and harder and act more and more outrageously. "You want a little bit of this?" Sally asked James, and turned Laura around, bending her at the waist. Suddenly, it wasn't so funny to Laura, as she felt herself get incredibly wet nearly instantaneously. To have Robert look at her that way was something she desired so much, and knowing James would take the lead would maybe free Robert up to be more obvious about his desires. Besides, James still had those damned gloves on.

It was only natural for Sally to spank her next—how could she not?—and the heat she felt on her ass turned her on even more. She wasn't wearing panties—she had gone without to surprise Robert at the end of the night—and instead she was surprising herself.

While the girls were turning each other on in their exhibitionist frenzy, something really odd had happened on the couch. James had put one of his leather-clad hands on his own package, and with the other—unconscious of what he was doing—was stroking Robert's nylon-clad leg. Robert was so turned on by his girlfriend's beautiful ass, and so shocked and thrilled to watch it being spanked by a gorgeous, half-naked girl, he hadn't even noticed. In fact, he didn't notice how much he enjoyed the feeling, either. Nor did James. So the two of them sat on the couch, oblivious of the lines they had crossed—which is probably the only way they could have crossed them.

They weren't about to notice, either, because just then Sally started to lift Laura's skirt an inch at a time. Laura genuinely protested when she remembered she had no panties on, but Sally still thought she was fooling around, playing the part. It was only when she saw the look on the men's faces that she realized Laura had good reason to protest. She quickly dropped the skirt, pulled Laura upright, and apologized. "I'm sorry, honey." She squished up her face as if to say, "Please don't hate me" and bit her bottom lip. Laura was so turned on by being exposed and spanked that she just kissed Sally again. Sally knew immediately that this was no joke. She kissed her back.

Both men had a moment of shock. This was no show anymore, not for them: Their girlfriends were really kissing. James grew possessive and stood up, grabbing Robert by the arm as he did so, forcing him to stand up, too. "Back to the original lesbians," he said, and he pulled Sally from Laura and pushed Robert into her place.

Laura was lit by lust as well as alcohol. She didn't rest a minute but kissed Robert full on. He was overwhelmed, excited, turned on: Sally and Robert were on the couch now, watching, Sally with one hand distractedly on her stomach, James's hand on her knee.

Laura grabbed her boyfriend's ass and pulled him close to her so she could feel his erection and hide it—because she knew he was shy about stuff like that—from Sally and James. She took over Sally's lead. "You want to see a really beautiful ass?" Without waiting for an answer, she whipped Robert around and bent him over. She didn't know if she was feeling motivated to share her exhibitionist turn-on with Robert or if she was just humiliating him, and she didn't care. She crouched down to his ankles and slid her hands up his nyloned legs, letting her nails slide against them and pulling his skirt up as she stood. He did have a beautiful ass, and with his boyish long legs, he was the perfect androgyne. James and Sally were still watching, fascinated by this crossdressed man who looked like a woman. Seeing him be objectified by his own girlfriend was, well, hot.

Robert was hard as a rock despite himself. Laura's powerful lust and her nails against his legs were turning him on, but when she pulled his skirt to his waist and bent him over like Sally had done to her, he nearly came on the spot. He had never felt so turned on, and the idea of Sally and James watching, looking at him sexually as if he were the girl, and Laura treating him like a girl—it was all too much.

He let her do whatever she wanted, and thought to himself that finally she had figured out what turned him on: not being a girl per se but being submissive, doing whatever she wanted. Laura knew it, she had always known it, and she was turned on by how powerful she was feeling, treating him that way. She spanked his ass and made him spread his legs a little farther apart as she ran her hands up the inside of his thighs and felt up between them for his hard cock. She stroked him a few times and he gasped. He'd come, just like that.

Sally got up and took Robert's hand, sitting him down on the couch with her and James. Laura stood there, the only one onstage, disgusted with how quickly Robert had come. He was not the type to recharge quickly, especially when he was drunk, and she had to get laid. She was over-the-top horny, having touched Sally's bare breasts and felt James's eyes on her, so she stood there for a minute not really knowing what to do.

She didn't say a word but looked at all three of them on the couch and started primly unbuttoning her skirt at the waist. She let it drop when she'd undone the hook and eye, and stood there, without panties, in a white garter belt and stockings. Her dark kitty was trim, and the insides of her thighs were slick. She was still wearing the corset that pinched her waist and gave her cleavage, and she wasn't about to take it off. She just stood there, looking at Robert as if to say, "This is what you can't fuck now," and at Sally as if to say, "This is what you've done," and lastly at James. Sally swallowed hard and got up.

"C'mere, honey," she said as she first took Laura's hands and then her arms and then hugged her. Laura hugged her back but she'd never been with a woman, she didn't know what to do next, and all the playfulness that had given her license to play with Sally before was gone. "C'mere, honey," Sally said again, and this time she looked at James. She'd been talking to James the whole time, but no one but Sally had known it. James stood up, his cock hard under his jeans, and waited for Sally's directions.

Sally pulled out of the hug and took Laura's hands again. She looked into her eyes and kissed her, and Laura nearly cried with the realization that Sally knew exactly how she felt, how much she wanted a man, not a man who was more like a woman than anything else. She wanted someone to take charge of her, to want her and possess her. It was just a momentary exchange between the two women, but it was all there.

James finally realized what was going on and nearly had a heart attack. He started to unbutton his jeans, when Laura stood back up quickly and turned around to do it, instead. Sally had sat back down on the couch with Robert, where she helped him get his heels and hose and panties off. She put his head on her shoulder and sometimes held and sometimes stroked his now limp cock. She put her other hand in her own lap and masturbated herself while they watched Laura undo James's zipper, pull down the front of his underwear, and hold his hard cock. She leaned over and kissed him once, deeply, and then turned back around, pulling up against him to feel her naked ass against his heat. He fished a condom out of his jeans, put it on, and before entering her asked, "What do you want, Laura? What do you want from me?"

Laura looked at Sally and Robert. Robert started to get up, and Sally pushed him back down. "Just watch her," she whispered into his ear, "and look at how beautiful she is." Robert couldn't help it. Laura was the most beautiful woman in the world to him, and he always came so fast because she turned him on so much.

"What do you want, Laura?" James said again.

"I want you to fuck me," she said, closing her eyes, and she felt Robert's eyes on her more keenly than she felt the cock that slid inside her.

MORE THAN MEETS THE EYE

Stephen Albrow

My suit is by Giorgio Armani, but my underwear is by Victoria's Secret. The boss wants me to play hardball today, to be at my most masculine, so I need something soft and sensuous against my skin to keep me in touch with the real me, with Suzy. I spent two hours in the shower this morning, shaving every last trace of hair from my body while going through the numbers in my head. The boss wants to secure the takeover deal for £2.5 million at the most, but I reckon I can snare them for 1.75, if I push hard enough. Yeah, I've got to be a tough guy today—at least, on the outside. Today, I'll be a tough guy in white satin bra and panties, with matching garter belt and tan stockings (fully fashioned, naturally!).

I blend in with the boardroom easily enough, with its ultra-masculine oak-paneled walls and high-back leather chairs. There are ten of us seated round the negotiating table, five of them and five of us. We're all wearing matching charcoal-gray suits because that's what the well-dressed man is wearing this year.

Only one person in the room breaks the dull, gray monotony—the power-dressed lady sitting directly to my right. She crosses her legs, which makes her skirt ride up and reveal several inches of stocking-clad thigh. Her stockings are the same shade of tan as mine, but hers aren't fully fashioned. She's on their side and she talks quite a lot. She and my boss make all the introductions, while I wait patiently for my moment—the moment when the number crunching begins.

A huge piece of my future will be decided by how well I function today, so I can feel myself getting nervous. The negotiations have been friendly so far, like they always are when two companies first sound each other out. But then it gets to the money shot, and when the money comes in, the warmth ships out. The boss is making a very long speech, one I've heard him practice many times before, so I zone right out from what he's saying and cross my legs like the lady just did because I know how good it must have felt to her. Nothing beats feeling two stocking-clad thighs brushing against each other in the tight confines of a miniskirt, but my charcoal-gray pants kill the moment for me because I don't feel the kiss of nylon on nylon.

Envious, I gaze down at the lady's legs, then down at my own for comparison's sake. She's wearing killer heels, which expose her toes, but her nails aren't painted—not red, like mine. It seems that some women don't want to make the effort. I guess they don't know how lucky they are. She gets to expose what I have to keep hidden—and the bitch doesn't even bother to paint her toenails!

A hissy fit wells inside me at the sheer injustice of it all, so I slip my hand inside my jacket. My Brooks Brothers shirt is thick enough to cover up my white satin bra and garter belt, but not so thick that I can't feel the garter belt's lace trim as I run a fingertip over my abs. Just knowing this little bit of Suzy is there, just making this little bit of contact with her, is enough to soothe my anger and calm my nerves. I zone back in on what the boss is saying, then their CEO gets to have his say.

"It's a great honor for a firm such as ours to be holding talks with a firm such as yours," he begins, which is the cue for me to zone out again. The meeting started twenty minutes ago, and everyone is still making nice with each other. But eventually they'll cut to the chase, the numbers guys will step in, and things will turn nasty.

The woman by my side crosses her legs again, pulling at her hem to stop her skirt riding up any farther, so I wait for a moment and then copy her actions. Trying to imagine my pants aren't there, I place my left leg on top of the right. And though I don't get to feel my nylons coming magically together in a silky kiss, the action does make my pants go tight around my thighs, producing a protruding line from hip to mid-thigh—a garter mark poking through the charcoal gray.

I keep it there for as long as I dare, soothed by this visible glimpse of Suzy. A part of me wants to reach down and stroke it, but I'm scared of drawing attention to myself. My boss is seated just inches away from me, near enough to see for sure what it is because the metal clip where it fixes to the stocking is clearly outlined. Basically, it's unmistakable! I turn toward their CEO, just acting casual, but already I'm feeling a stirring in my crotch. My arousal stems from a contradiction—the contradiction that governs my life as Suzy: The delicious fear of being found out fights my burning desire for them all to know.

My fear wins out, as it always does, so I uncross my legs and let my pants hang loose. I think of the thousands of times I've sat at my desk with Suzy hidden beneath my suit. Every day I'm kind of hoping there'll be some way to bring her out in the open, but every day I leave relieved to know my secret's still intact. It's my own little game, my own private area of self-expression. Do I really want to be a woman, turning up in skirts every day, or does the thrill come from wearing what I'm not meant to wear? Would my nylons hold the same appeal for me if I didn't have to keep them tucked out of sight? Or is this whole thing just a way for me to rebel against the dull conformity of charcoal gray?

The lady by my side is talking again, giving us a few too many details about her firm's carbon emissions. My boss pretends to show concern, but I can see the pound signs in his eyes. We're in the moneymaking business; we're not doing this to save the world. I can see what he's thinking: *Lady, you can shove your carbon emissions right back up your ass.*

He turns to me and winks conspiratorially, which for some odd reason makes me blush. I quickly work out why—because I'm feeling kind of Suzy, and it's like he's just seen me in my lingerie. My Armani suit hangs limp and loose on me, but the satin and hose cling so tightly to my body. My stockings are like a second skin, molded perfectly to fit my legs, while my panties and bra feel more like a warm embrace than clothing. These undergarments feel so sensuous, so right on my body, but I'm not in contact with the suit at all. It's really just an outer shell; I can easily forget it's even there.

I turn to the woman, more than ever aware of the contradiction within me. Everything about her matches, from her skirt to her stockings to her female heart, whereas I'm in three layers—first, the manly suit and, second, the girlie underwear and, after that, a soul that was born to be one thing but wants to be another and that ends up stuck there, somewhere in between.

For a moment, I'm struck with a bitter, chilling sense of my own absurdity as I imagine the woman hitching up her skirt to expose a pair of boxer shorts. It doesn't make for a pretty picture; in fact, it seems ridiculous, but maybe that's for the simple reason that men's underwear is so functional and bland. Were a guy to take a beautiful woman home and find her underwear doesn't match the glamour of her outerwear, it could only lead to disappointment. But Suzy offers something special, like a piece of dark chocolate with a soft, gooey center. The magic is on the inside; bite through the outer layer and the fun begins. Uncovering beautiful lingerie could never be a disappointment, and maybe it's even more exciting when the outer shell holds so little promise.

The bitter chill passes through me quickly, and once again I feel secure in my own form of femininity. I picture myself standing in front of the mirror that morning, before Armani came along and spoiled the lady-like view. Then I ask myself what underwear the woman has on and whether she gets the same kick out of it as I always do. My guess is she's wearing pantyhose, not stockings, with a black bra and panties to match her skirt and jacket. She smiles at me as she reels off some statistics, and I realize she's very attractive. As a guy, I would definitely fancy her, but today we're in competition. We both want to be the sexiest lady in the boardroom and, anyway, Suzy's not into girls. She likes manly hands on her stocking-clad thighs, hands that can make her feel all woman.

I turn to Jeff, their moneyman, with whom I'll be doing battle any moment now. He's sitting directly across from me, and when I glance at him, he looks away. I'd caught him looking and the momentary eye contact seems to have embarrassed him, as it would if you'd been spotted staring at someone you were attracted to. *Perhaps he likes me,* I start to think, then he looks straight back and grins at me. He casts his eyes up and down my body, like he's mentally undressing me. Not stripping me naked, but just ripping away the Armani shell and feasting his eyes on the shaven flesh encased in crisp white satin and fully fashioned nylon.

I blush again, wondering if he's spotted a bra strap or something, but everything's hidden safely beneath my suit. It's possible he's just trying to psyche me out, but somehow I don't think
so. There's a warmth coming off him, as if he genuinely likes me.
I've never believed in love at first sight, but sexual attraction can
happen in an instant, so I start to wonder if Jeff might be gay.
Has the sexual predator inside him somehow sensed my inner
submissiveness, as witnessed by my need to sheathe my masculine form in come-and-get-me frills?

The lady stops speaking, and the moment arrives for Jeff and
me to write down our figures and push them across the table.
I put our offer in an envelope, then slide it toward him like a
teenager passing a love note in class. It's a devilishly flirty process, especially when our fingers touch, as I take his envelope
in return. My poker face is on, so I don't bridle at his opening
gambit, which is 250K above the maximum we're willing to pay.
I whisper to my boss while Jeff whispers to his, aware of the
mounting tension in the room. Everything that's happened till
now has only been so much talk. Everyone else is irrelevant now.
It's just Jeff and me and our respective bosses.

The lady starts examining a manicured nail as I write my second offer down. Like a schoolgirl cheating on a math exam, she
tries to take a peek at my paper, but I quickly fold it and place it
in an envelope. Jeff is taking his time on this one, unaware that
I've moved straight in for the kill, presenting him with a take-it-
or-leave-it offer. I'm playing hardball, that's for sure, because I
know we're in the box seat. I feel bad in a way, but it's my job to
be bad, and my underwear hugs me, allowing me to be so bad.
Only by being at my most feminine underneath am I able to be
so hard on the outside.

Everyone is staring at Jeff now, waiting for his envelope to
join mine in the center of the table. His CEO folds his arms

across his chest, his body language getting defensive. He knows he pitched his opening figure way too high, which has allowed me to finish this off so fast. I already know that they'll agree to my second offer of £1.75 million, with a couple of sweeteners thrown in to secure the deal. In the end, Jeff doesn't even put up a counterpunch. He just picks up my envelope, then shakes my hand. He's been pussy whipped by a guy in stockings, but I know I can make it up to him. In fact, I *have* to make it up to him because I've just been knocked completely off balance.

A wave of testosterone courses through my veins, as everyone rushes to slap me on the back. The lady kisses both my cheeks, then her CEO puts his hand on my shoulder. He tells me what a great deal I've done, but I'm distracted by how close his index finger is to touching my bra strap. I take all the congratulations on offer, but a part of me wants to get out of there because I'm overdosing on masculinity. They're all telling me what a hard bargain I drove, but I'm not the man they think I am. I don't like the role that they're making me play. I desperately need to redress the balance.

"You sure don't pull any punches," says Jeff, shaking my hand and not letting go. I'm relieved to see his face in the crowd because he seems to see right through me. He wants my ass, I'm sure of that now. I'm sure he's sensed the woman within me.

"Thanks," I tell him, then I jump as a champagne cork pops. Drinks are handed out to everyone, so Jeff and I clink glasses and take a sip. Our roles in the proceedings are over now—now it's all in the hands of the legal teams—so I'm happy to see the champagne flowing freely. I chat with Jeff, getting drunk very quickly, liking how fast our positions have reversed. As a negotiator, I was in full control, but now he's taking charge of things, dominating the conversation like a good man should. Flirty and witty, he sucks the testosterone out of my veins, making me feel like a shy, awkward girl desperately in need of a date for prom night.

I need to be female, to burst out of my shell, and somehow Jeff seems to know that. Just like I knew how badly his company needed this deal, allowing me to play hardball with him, so Jeff is aware of my desperation to girl it up, which means he's certain to have my ass. I'm cozying up to him like a bitch in heat, laughing at all his wisecracks and practically batting my eyelashes at him. The cold-eyed determination with which I faced him across the negotiating table has vanished into thin air now. My delicate underwear is hugging my torso, but Giorgio Armani is nowhere. I feel certain Jeff can me see me in my full, feminine glory, because even *I* have lost sight of my masculinity now, as if my outer shell had been stripped away.

"This champagne goes right through me," says Jeff. Then he asks me where the washroom is.

"It goes right through me, too," I say. Then I tell my boss that Jeff and I are going to my office to work on some taxation issues. The boardroom is clearing out now anyway. The celebrations are coming to a close, and everyone is heading back to their departments to figure out how the takeover will work in practice. I grab my briefcase, then ask Jeff to follow me. It's an effort not to wiggle my butt for him as I lead him to the executive washroom.

We both know what we're headed there for, so Jeff doesn't flinch when I put up the notice. There's a No Entry – Cleaning in Progress sign kept just inside the door, so I hang it on the outside handle and shut us in. "You must've done this before," he says, as he gets close enough for me to smell his cologne. His chin is stubbled, in contrast to mine, which, like my body, is smooth as silk.

"Oh, this girl's been around the block," I say, as he leans

toward me and kisses my mouth. He's taller than me, with a better-developed upper body than mine, which heightens my feeling of femininity. As his tongue parts my lips, I let him ease me out of my jacket, and then he tugs my shirt out of my pants. Either he can't wait to get me naked or he knows there's something hidden underneath. Whichever—he'll find out my secret soon enough because his hands are up my shirt now, where they touch the bare flesh between my bra and garter belt. Slowly, his fingers creep up my back, till they touch my satin bra strap. Right then, Jeff's kiss seems to miss a beat, but he's quickly back on top of things.

My secret is out in the open now, and I feel myself melting into Jeff's muscular embrace. I grow dizzy, light-headed, as if I'm no longer able to bear my own body weight. I need a good, strong man to carry me, and I'm lucky enough to have found one in Jeff. His tongue is still inside my mouth, and his hands are now exploring the rest of my body, pushing down the back of my pants to grab hold of my satin-covered buns. I unzip my fly and watch the charcoal-gray fabric slump around my ankles, exposing my nylons, which Jeff instantly gropes. His hands slide up and down the backs of my thighs with an assuredness that surprises me. It's as if he'd always known he'd find a woman underneath. It's as if Suzy had been radiating out to him throughout the meeting.

I crook my right thigh, pressing it tight against Jeff's hip, which makes it easier for him to reach my stocking top and butt. Our crotches come together, allowing me to feel the growing stiffness in his dick. I can feel my cock trying to lengthen, too, but it's tucked away inside my frilly white panties. Stuffed between my legs, it jerks and throbs, but it has no room in which to rise and ruin my bulge-free front. I am completely emasculated, female to the core. The outer me and the inner me are now as one.

I lift up my arms so Jeff can pull off my shirt, then I kick off my shoes and step out of my pants. Kneeling down, I peel off my socks, then I open up my briefcase and take out a pair of open-toe stilettos. Jeff watches as I slip them on, then helps me to my feet and follows me over to the washbasins. I set down my briefcase on the marble ledge and then gaze into the mirrored wall. I haven't bought much makeup with me—just some lipstick, mascara, eye shadow. and rouge—but it's enough to turn me into Suzy.

Jeff stands behind me, gazing over my shoulder, watching my reflection switch from male to female. He kisses my neck, then his hands reach round my torso and his fingers touch my empty bra cups. I don't know if he's gay or bi, or whether chicks with dicks are his *thang* at all, but he's clearly transfixed by my transformation. Probably he'd just prefer me as a guy, but he seems willing to go along for the ride. His dick is pressed tight against the back of my panties, and his erection shows no sign of going limp.

Fully made up, I reach into my briefcase and then lower Suzy's hair down onto my head. The long, brunette wig tumbles halfway down my torso, submerging my flesh in a sea of soft, feminizing curls. My reflection excites me, so I catch Jeff's eye in the mirror and then ask him, huskily, how I look. He thinks for a bit, then answers, "Kinky!" Liking his response, I stick out my tush and start bucking my buns against his long, thick dick.

I'm leaning forward now, my hands upon the marble ledge, watching both Jeff and the female me reflected in the mirror. His breath warms my shoulders as he leans right around and tastes the lipstick on my mouth. His hands move from my bra to my thighs, sliding over my garter belt and then tugging down my tight, white panties. They drop to the floor, leaving my cock-hungry asshole completely exposed. I take some lube from my briefcase and pass it back to my hunky lover.

Jeff unzips his fly and drops his pants to reveal his own little underwear secret. He prefers not to wear any, prefers to go commando, so straightaway I get to see how huge his dick is. Staring at me in the mirror, he smears his cock with a blob of lube, then squirts another dollop between my buns. I gasp as he uses a fingertip to work the gunk into my rectal cavity. He's gentle with his finger, but when his cockhead slips inside me, he fucks me like the two-bit whore I am.

Jeff grips his fingers hard into my thighs, then starts ramming his cock in and out of my ass. The muscles in my anal passage don't seem to know what's hit them. Every forward thrust is over eight inches deep—hard enough and deep enough to make me squeal like a virgin bride. I watch myself in the mirror, see the squeals of pleasure bursting out of my crimson lips, happy and excited to be bent over and fucked hard and deep like a proper girl. The masculine me shafted Jeff in the boardroom, but now he's the one shafting me. I might have seemed like a real man at the negotiating table, but now my true colors are coming out—coming out of my hose and heel-filled closet!

Jeff's full length slams inside my anus, knocking me forward with the force of the thrust. Beads of perspiration pour off his forehead, landing on my naked back and chasing one another toward my ass like raindrops on a windowpane. The hot, sweaty moisture sends excited shivers through my flesh, which echo the sex-induced pulsations in my anus. I grab my cock, which is now standing upright, and squeeze my fingers around the tip. I feel my crown throbbing, just like my butthole, as the tension inside me drives me wild.

I stare in the mirror, gazing up and down my body, which appears to be that of a genuine girl. Was it really me that cut that deal? Was it really me in that charcoal-gray suit? They tell me it was, but all I can see is a pretty girl, her clothes ripped off, just her underwear remaining, and a tall, strong lover standing proud behind her, driving his enflamed dick in and out of her rear-entry hole. I blink, but the image doesn't change. It still tallies with the image of me that I've always had inside my head. I'm jerking off hard now, just thinking of it…how I've become the girl I always wanted to be. Sure, I did the man bit earlier, but sexy, flirty Suzy is back. Playing hardball in the boardroom—that was only make-believe. Jeff has brought the real me back, redressing the balance with his rock-hard dick, using his sexual magic to turn the testosterone that surged through my veins into 100 percent pure estrogen.

He's been fucking me hard now for many minutes, but I'm the one who lets out the climactic yell. All the nerve endings in my anus have been overstimulated by his massive prick, so now my prostate gland is twitching like mad and my crown is pulsing in my hand. I jerk once more, then feel the cream squirting out between the cracks in my fingers, propelled by a sequence of gut-churning spasms inside my head. A sexual fire blazes throughout my feminized body, stretching as high as my curly tresses and down as far as my painted toenails. The fire rages within me, then rages on, the blistering heat never seeming to fade, not even minutes later. My dick might not be throbbing anymore, and the well of my seed may now have run dry, but this orgasm goes way beyond the purely physical. Like a true female, I experience a climax of the mind, which multiplies endlessly as Jeff continues to screw my ass.

His thrusts are gradually slowing now, turning sharper and more forceful. Tightening my sphincter muscles around his length, I can feel the signs of his imminent orgasm. Pulsations of pleasure make his prickhead spasm, so he pulls right back and then hammers home. His meaty erection splits my orifice down the center, plugging up my body with a defiant show of masculine force. Submissive to the end, I bend over farther and accept the spunk that he shoots up my ass. Goose bumps break out all over my body, as his orgasmic pulsations reverberate though my anal walls. Next, his hands reach for my thighs and touch my silky stocking tops. He seems to like the womanly texture of my nylons, because his dick throbs even harder and another thick wave of spunk pours out.

We freeze in this tableau in front of the mirror, half-smiling at each other in the glass. Jeff's breathing is heavy, which suggests he's tired, but his cock still bursts with abundant life. I feel it, big and hard, inside me, pulsing in time with my anal throbs, until eventually Jeff withdraws from my anus, pulls up his pants, and kisses my lips. His tongue slides deep inside my mouth, the masculine aggressor again on the charge. I love him taking control like this because it feels so real to me. I'm myself for once, not playing a role like I was in the boardroom. When he strokes my girlie locks and pats me gently on the backside, I even wish they all could see. Yeah, I want them all to see me playing kitten with my man, but none of them will ever know.

"I better get back," Jeff says, and I agree, so he heads off out of the washroom. I stay in front of the mirror and wash all trace of Suzy from my face, before placing her wig back into my briefcase, along with her heels and her slutty tube of lube. I tuck my prick between my legs and then pull up my panties, ready to put my suit back on. Suzy gets covered in charcoal gray. They'll never know. My secret is safe. When I leave the washroom, they'll never know.

I walk back out into the office building, people scurrying all around me. No one gives me a second glance because no one can see through charcoal gray. Only I know I'm wearing fully fashioned stockings. Only I can feel the freshly fucked tingle in my ass.

I head for my desk, kind of pleased that no one notices anything untoward about me because that means I can keep on playing my private game. I'll let them think I'm a regular guy—conservative manner, conservative suit—but the truth is I have hidden depths. I'm more exciting than they think, a sexy special creature, most special of all because I keep it all hidden. White bra, matching panties, painted toenails, shaved legs. No, I'm not just another Armani clone. There's more to me than meets the eye.

TOUGH ENOUGH TO WEAR A DRESS

Teresa Noelle Roberts

The boutique owner approached me as I entered. "May I help you?"

For a moment, my surroundings didn't register very much because all I could see was her. She was built like a goddess—tall and extra curvy—and dressed like a forties movie star in a nipped-waisted suit that accented all those tasty curves and made everything else look sleek and airbrushed because it fit so perfectly. Her hair looked like auburn silk, and my fingertips burned to touch it.

I was so dazed that she had to repeat her question.

"I hear you might be able to make me something…" My voice trailed off as I looked from the gorgeous creature around her shop.

I was a bull dyke in a china shop, a jeans-and-Docs-clad intruder in femme heaven. Amazing evening gowns hung everywhere, interspersed with more vintage-inspired outfits like the one the auburn-haired goddess wore.

Clearly I'd come to the wrong place.

I backed toward the door like Wile E. Coyote trying to back-pedal through a wall.

Ridiculous what a sense of panic welled up just being sur-rounded by all the feminine accoutrements. I loved seeing other women wearing pretty, girly clothes—but for me? No way. I'd faced down a mugger once with no weapon other than bravado and that had set my heart racing less than the mere idea of wear-ing a dress.

She laughed, a throaty, erotic chuckle that seemed as film noir as her outfit. "Don't worry. I can see you're not the evening-gown type, although I have to say you have the figure for it, with that cleavage and that tiny waist and that round..."

"Okay, I *know* I have a big butt. Don't rub it in!"

"It's not big. It's delicious. You're built like Jessica Rabbit."

"Body of Jessica Rabbit, heart of a butch. It makes it hard to buy clothes off the rack." She was obviously flirting with me—and I was more than happy to flirt back—so why deny what she'd clearly already figured out?

"I'm Kate, the owner of Kate's Creations." She extended her hand to me.

I didn't quite kiss it, but the way I bowed over it let her know I was thinking of it. Not something I'd always do, but it seemed to go with her retro look.

"Andie Pace. I'm a fundraiser at the hospital—and I'm tired of renting tuxedos that never fit me for our black-tie events. One of my volunteers recommended you for custom tailoring."

Kate closed her eyes for a moment, and when she opened them again, I could tell she'd seen a vision. "Not a tuxedo, ex-actly," she said. "A man's vintage suit, but one custom made for your body. Very Marlene Dietrich."

What I knew about contemporary fashion could fit on a

penny, with room left over for something interesting, like a hot woman's phone number in very tiny type, but I know my old movies. I nodded eagerly. Marlene in a suit, looking all hot and gender-bending, was my idea of the perfect evening look. "There's just one condition," she said in a conspiratorial whisper. "The suit's got to make its first appearance on a date with me. It just seems a shame to waste it on a crowd that won't fully appreciate it—or the butch wearing it."

That had been four months ago, and since then my Marlene suit and I had enjoyed ourselves thoroughly, escorting delicious Kate to dinner, to the theater in New York City and Boston, to a holiday drag show in P'town—and to play parties in all sorts of places.

Both Kate and I were pure sensation players, not into role-play or power exchange, just pleasurable pain and edgy pleasure. She was more a top and I more a bottom, but we weren't hidebound about that. We both, as it turned out, had a bit of an exhibitionist streak. And when we showed up at a play party, I in the Marlene suit and she in whatever one of her femmelicious creations she was wearing that particular night, women's heads turned, assuring we'd get a good audience.

And then the time came for the New England Fetish Festival.

We'd each attended it before on our own, but the idea of going with Kate made my pulse race and my pussy throb. Three days at a hotel with the sexiest and sweetest woman I'd ever dated, surrounded by a bunch of fun, kinky people. Lots of play parties. Lots of new toys to check out (I love toys). And, since Kate loves any opportunity to play dress-up and I love any opportunity to appear in public with her on my arm, lots of chances to parade around in our best fetish wear.

For Kate, the highlight of the Fetish Festival is the Saturday masquerade ball. For the past month, she'd been working late nights at the shop, finishing up a vinyl version of Edwardian evening wear, and I was dying to see her in it—I knew it would be killer with her curvy, girly figure. My fetish wardrobe was much more limited than hers, but the way I saw it, as the butch my job is to look tough yet cute and not upstage her. I planned to throw all my variations on the theme of black leather into my suitcase, along with the Marlene suit, and have her help me put together outfits that wouldn't embarrass her in public.

By the time the Saturday evening of the event rolled around, our hotel room was a chaotic pit of clothes, shopping bags, and toys of various sorts, and it smelled like a busy day at the bordello. First, we'd gotten a new flogger and clover nipple clips and had to test them out on me. Then we'd found a new dildo for my strap-on rig and had to test that on Kate. (Both sets of purchases worked scream-inducingly well.) Then we ran into some friends who'd just bought their first cane and wanted pointers on how to use it. Kate was happy to demonstrate, using me as a stunt butt. (In my opinion, the only thing more fun than a good caning is a good caning with an attractive and appreciative audience.)

I floated on the endorphins from that scene all the way through dinner, getting a fresh hit every time I squirmed in my seat—and trust me, I was squirming in my seat deliberately, feeling that lovely, painful afterglow and anticipating more action later.

Especially when Kate whispered something about wanting me to wear the strap-on to the party.

I don't usually pack. For me, the fun of packing would be all about sexual opportunism, but the squishy packing dildos that look like actual relaxed boy-bits are no good for fucking—and bit of an exhibitionist or not, I'm not about to go most places in the everyday world with a silicone stiffy at my crotch. In this setting, though, it could be entertaining, if it amused Kate, and apparently it did.

Had she gotten invites to a private play party? Did she want to sneak off and have a quickie in a dark corner of the ballroom? (The masquerade was supposedly a no-genital-sex zone, but late enough in the evening, no one really cared.) Or would we just be teasing each other all evening long, her body pressing against my artificial dick until we were both insane with need?

The possibilities left me wet and thrumming with lust by the time we went up to change.

We knew we'd never leave the room if we got into the shower together—a tempting thought, but Kate had worked so hard on her dress that I wanted her to have a chance to show it off—so I claimed the bathroom first, knowing I'd be out quickly and could dress and read a couple of chapters of the latest Stephanie Plum mystery while Kate put together an outfit for me.

When I got out of the bathroom, though, there was something very wrong spread on the bed for me to put on.

A dress or, to be more specific, an evening gown.

A damn gorgeous gown, all burgundy velvet and slink and swagger. I could easily imagine the cleavage-enhancing, waist-flattering, butt-cupping, torso-lengthening magic it would work on some other woman.

But I knew it wasn't for some other woman.

Not when my new dildo and my jaunty "cowgirl"-model leather harness were laid out on top of it, and my knee-high Docs, polished to a mirror shine, were at the foot of the bed.

At least she wasn't trying to get me into girly shoes, I thought as the panic rose in my throat, threatening to bring dinner with it. "No," I managed to choke out, and the word took on three or four syllables as nerves made me stutter.

Kate, naked and ready for the shower by this time, folded her arms around me. "Andie, sweetie, it's just fabric. A costume for the masquerade. It doesn't change who you are. I'd love to see you in it, but you don't have to."

I burrowed into the warmth between her breasts, breathing in her exotic spicy perfume, the smell of sex, the smell of comfort. Face safely pressed against Kate, I couldn't see the dress taunting me anymore, couldn't see the memories that went with it.

She was right, of course. But logic had very little to do with what I was feeling, with the wave of memories threatening to drown me.

"Did you know," I said, talking to my lady's beautiful breasts because I was afraid to meet the nonexistent eyes of a formal gown, "that I was one of the candidates for prom queen back in high school?"

"You? My tomboy Andie?"

Despite the weird way I was feeling, I could only laugh at the incredulity in her voice. "I was one of the popular girls back then. The other girls liked me because I was funny and because I'd attract boys' attention and then let my friends flirt with them. Like a bait and switch to get customers in the door, you know. They got extra boys, and I got to hang out with the cheerleaders in their little short skirts and go into dressing rooms at the mall with the hottest girls in school. Stuff like that. So, anyway, prom night 1988 in a small town in New Hampshire. Picture me with big hair."

"And lots of ruffles, I bet."

"Bright turquoise ones. But the ruffles were all on the bottom, and the dress showed off my cleavage, and I guess I looked pretty good. Good enough that one of the other candidates decided to tell everyone I was a lesbian so people wouldn't vote for me."

I took a deep breath, remembering a night I'd thought I'd blocked out pretty thoroughly as if it were yesterday. "Which I could have dealt with. Hell, I could have batted my eyes at a couple of boys and everyone would have been like, 'Oh, Mary Ellen's just jealous—Andrea's so not a lezbo.' But my mom was one of the chaperones that night and someone was dumb enough to do her rumor-mongering in the bathroom—where my mom was at the time. I could lie to the entire high school but not to my mom."

"So after semipublic humiliation you got to have one of those awful talks with your family?"

"Make it a huge fight with my family, the kind where my father didn't speak to me for about a month except to say, 'Pass the ketchup.' They've come around okay, but it hit them from completely out of left field. I'd tried to fit in, done all the standard girl things—they kept saying a pretty girl like me, a girl with a closet full of nice clothes and shoes, couldn't be a lesbian."

"Guess they'd never heard of femmes," Kate said dryly, then kissed the top of my head, ruffling my short-cropped hair in the process. "I'm sorry about surprising you with the dress, sweetie. I just thought I might be a fun thing to do for the masquerade."

"I've never really talked about it to anyone. It was too painful and too stupid at the same time. All that public drama and I hadn't even kissed a girl yet! But once everyone including my parents knew..." I took a deep breath. "Well, I just stopped trying to fit in, just put my head down, graduated, and headed to college for the summer session instead of waiting until fall. And once I got to school, I decided no one was going to be able to blackmail me about being queer again because I was going to make it obvious. First, I got my hair cut. Then, I went to a consignment shop and traded in all my girl clothes for a leather biker jacket and some boots. And then I went looking for the lesbian and bi women's group on campus."

Kate didn't say anything, just lifted my chin and pulled me into a dizzying kiss, a kiss into which she seemed to pouring her whole heart and all her feelings.

Her hands snaked their way down my back, awakening the skin behind them, to cup my ass cheeks. Knowing how I liked mixed-up sensations—a little pain with my pleasure, a little edge with my tenderness—she pinched at the fiery little welts left behind from the afternoon's adventures.

Yeah, she knew me all right, knew the best way to distract me from difficult memories (or from just about anything else that might be bothering me) was with sensation, with sex. I fell into the kiss, opened my legs to give her hands access to my sudden wetness, let my hands roam over her silken skin.

She didn't give me a chance to do much to her but backed me up onto the other bed, the one that didn't have our dresses spread out, the one that was already pretty much destroyed by sex, and pushed me down onto it.

Kisses and bites. Caresses alternating with sharp slaps on my thighs and already tender nipples, just hard enough to be punctuation. No toys, although we had a room full of them, just Kate's lips, Kate's teeth, Kate's clever hands. My brain shut off, focused only on the pleasure and the pain, on the fire and need building between my legs, on the feel and smell and miracle that was Kate.

I can't take her whole hand without lube and a lot of time, and we didn't have a lot of time, but three fingers ground into me easily, and then she worked her mouth down to move in concert, and I screamed loudly enough that they probably heard me back in my old hometown, let alone in the next room, and bucked and convulsed around her hand.

And as my head cleared, it really cleared. I figured something
out that I probably should have figured out about twenty years
ago. "Stupid to blame the clothes, isn't it? I was hiding behind
them, but they're just clothes. If I wear a dress with the right attitude, everyone will know…"

Kate kissed me with lips that tasted of me. "That you're a dyke
in a costume," she finished for me. "A fabulous, flattering costume—but one that enhances who you are, instead of hiding it."

I glanced over gingerly at the other bed. At the dress, the
Docs, the strap-on. "Especially if I have a huge silicone cock
making a tent in the front of it," I said, laughing. "Sure, I'll give
it a try. But you're going to have to help me into it—and out of
it later."

"I will," she promised. "Besides—look." She pulled out her
garment bag and took out her outfit. "We'll both be in drag."

It was a vinyl Edwardian outfit, all right. A vinyl Edwardian
men's outfit, tailcoat and pants with the black-on-black stripes,
like a Merchant–Ivory film gone wildly askew.

I admit I followed her into the shower and tried to distract
her. I even succeeded for a few minutes, but we still made it to
the masquerade, Kate in her vinyl Edwardian splendor, I as Jessica Rabbit.

If you imagine Jessica Rabbit with short-cropped hair, big,
stompy boots, and a plunging neckline that drew all eyes to her
dick.

As we entered the room, someone whistled. Heads turned.

And while I still felt weird, I knew we looked good. Knew
that with our roles reversed so strikingly, in fact, we might look
better, or at least more head-turning, than ever.

Yeah, I thought, I'd pick me up if I were single. I'd pick Kate
up if she hadn't already picked me up.

At first, though, I hid on the sidelines, enjoying the heated, curious glances we were getting, but not sure how to dance in a long gown.

Then a slow, sultry song came on. Kate dragged me onto the dance floor, and I discovered I could dance no matter what I was wearing as long as I was dancing with her.

And when we made our way back to our room, I pulled my skirt up and then pulled Kate's trousers down, and I fucked her hard and deep, fucked her thoroughly, fucked her with velvet and vinyl caressing my skin and hers until we both saw stars.

A real butch—I decided as we curled up together, spent, in a heap of costumes that would need dry-cleaning and repair—is tough enough to put on a dress to please her lady.

At least if there's a strap-on involved.

THE SWEETHEART OF SIGMA QUEER

Simon Sheppard

"Suck my cock," I said, and he did. Not the best I've had, but good, very good, and anyway the whole situation kind of excited me. He opened wide and took my dick as far down his throat as he could. I moaned. His tongue did a little dance on the underside of my shaft, and this time I moaned for real.

"That's it," I said. "That's a good, hungry cocksucker." He nursed on my flesh a little more, then pulled away, raised himself up, threw his arms around me, kissed me on the lips. I kissed back.

"Hot," he said when the kiss had ended. "Really hot."

I like to know the guys I have sex with. It's a stupid trait, one that's gotten me into trouble any number of times, but there it is. "How'd you get into…"

"This?"

"Yeah, this," I said.

He lay back, one hand lazily stroking my damp hard-on.

"In high school I always felt like an outsider, and a queer

outsider at that. So when I went off to college, I wanted to feel like I belonged. I suppose I still do." He smiled up at me. "My dad had gone to the same university, and I really wanted to join the frat he'd been in. So I felt real lucky when, after the bid party, I was invited to pledge. The fraternity brothers were a bunch of straight guys, a lot of them jocks, and though I wasn't exactly that, I guess I passed."

He'd taken his hand off my hard-on. I guided it back and he jacked me off as he continued.

"There'd been a hazing scandal a couple of years before— somebody had nearly died—so the stuff we pledges were put through was more humiliating than anything else. You know the kind of thing: 'Turn around, drop your pants, and bend over.' It's a funny thing about mooning: It can be read as a sign of contempt, but it's also submissive behavior, proffering your ass to an alpha male."

The guy was an intellectual, no fucking doubt about that. I got my fingers wet with spit and reached down to his ass, proffered or not, and began to rub his softly puckered hole.

"Should I stop talking?"

"No, keep going," I said. What the hell.

He smiled and snuggled up to me, his hand still working my cock. "After the trou-dropping, the brothers brought out a box of women's lingerie and had us pledges strip down and put it on. We had to walk from the frat house to the quad that way. And back. I can remember what I had to wear: a silky black slip and matching panties.

"I guess I looked good in lingerie; I was accepted into the frat. I moved into a room with my Big Brother, Tony. He was a business major and kind of a jock, but not offensively so, and we got along just fine. In fact, the whole fraternity thing was pretty good. Sure, I was surrounded by straight boys and sure, some of them could be assholes, but most of them were nice. Of course, they didn't know I was queer. I was really closeted then and I wasn't about to let on to the brothers that I wanted to suck their dicks."

"There wasn't a gay frat on campus?" I asked.

"Honey, this was the Deep South, okay? Ten years ago."

"Okay." My fingers were pressing into his moist hole now. I wanted to fuck it. I wanted to fuck *him*.

"Then one night we held a big kegger. I admit it, I was pretty drunk. We all were. Over in one corner, Tony and his girlfriend were having what seemed like a heated argument; it looked like he wasn't going to get laid *that* night. Everybody else was dancing or groping or, like me, just chugging down brews. And a few of the brothers had stripped off their shirts, including this guy named Bret, all muscles and chin. I really had the hots for him. Okay, he was pretty much an unredeemable straight jerk, but with Bret I didn't want discourse, I wanted intercourse.

"With all that sweaty, liquored-up flesh around, I found myself with a fairly unmanageable hard-on, so I excused myself and went up to my room. I had just gotten down to jacking off when the door opened. Apparently, I'd been too blasted to properly lock it. It was my Big, Tony, and he'd caught me with my pants down. Literally. I didn't know what to expect, but I was a bit surprised when he just stood there with a big, drunken grin. Then he locked the door, unzipped his pants, and slurred, 'Do me, instead. I'm so fuckin' goddamn horny.' I'd seen him naked, of course, and I knew he had a nice cock, but I'd never seen it hard before. Now it was standing up like an open invitation, and it didn't take long for me to accept. Tony stood there for maybe a minute while I knelt, sucking him off, and then he gave a grunt, started pounding into my mouth, and came down my throat. I was still on my knees when he zipped back up, looking down at me with what probably was an appreciative smile—they do say that straight guys are the biggest fans of getting blown. Then he headed back to the party, leaving me and my hard-on to fend for ourselves."

He paused and looked at me uncertainly. I really wanted to put my dick inside him, but I also was a bit curious about what happened next. "What happened next?" I asked.

"Oh, Tony treated it like one of those 'Boy, was I drunk last night' things. But then I started servicing him on a regular basis. We never discussed it; I just sucked him off when he needed it. I hadn't had much sex before that, so it made me nervous, excited, and a bit ashamed, all rolled up into one. But I sure did like the fact that my roomie wanted to fuck my face.

"Then one night, shortly before Christmas break, when Tony had gone north on a weekend ski trip, there was a knock at my door. It was Bret, smelling like the Heineken brewery. 'Listen, Rick,' he said. And then nothing; the hunky guy was tongue-tied. At last he got it out: 'Don't get the wrong idea, okay? I'm straight, but...Well, Tony says you give the best blow jobs he's ever had.'

"I fucking almost fainted. I couldn't believe that my Big had told anyone about me. After all, it seemed like self-preservation would have meant his keeping quiet, right? But then I realized that if I was just a mouth to him, a mouth he could fuck, then he could get his rocks off and still keep his straight credentials intact. He could think of himself as a totally het boy who just liked being sucked off by another guy, and who knows, maybe he was. And now here was Bret, the muscled object of my fevered affections, and he wanted to be serviced, too. I know—if I had had a shred of self-respect, I probably would have said no. But, well, you know..."

"I think I do," I said, twisting two fingers inside his ass. Just how long was this story, anyway?

"I didn't say anything, so Bret must have figured—rightly, as it turned out—that I'd be happy to suck him off. He held out a gym bag he'd brought. 'Listen, can you put this stuff on? It will make it, um, easier for me,' he said, sounding more like a little boy than I'd have expected. Inside the bag was the black slip I'd worn during hazing. Not the black panties, though. The ones he'd brought were light-blue jobbies, very sheer. I couldn't believe it. See, what Bret couldn't have known, what I never would have told anyone, was that I'd found wearing lingerie exciting. Hazing was the first and only time I'd put on women's stuff, but on that walk through campus, I'd barely been able to keep my hard dick from jumping out of those panties. And in the months since I'd pledged, I'd often jacked off to thoughts of being naked except for silky underwear, surrounded by straight guys with hard dicks.

"So when Bret held out the lingerie, I eagerly stripped down, pulled on the slip and powder-blue panties, and got down on my knees. 'That's it,' Bret said. 'Suck me like a girl.' Bret's dick wasn't as prepossessing as the rest of his body, so even with my minimal experience I had no problem deep-throating him. He grabbed my head, muttered, "Eat it, bitch," and shot his load in my mouth. And that was that; I'd sucked off the man of my dreams. 'Put the clothes back in the bag,' he said. The slip was light as a cloud in my trembling hands. The crotch of the panties was soaked through. 'And don't,' he warned, 'tell anybody about this.' Like I would. After Bret left, I jacked off so hard my dick was sore all the next day."

He spit on his hand and went to work on my cock. It felt so damn good that my growing impatience vanished. Almost. But he wasn't finished talking yet.

"That was it. I didn't see Bret again before I left for winter break. I figured that he'd gotten himself some pussy and forgotten about me. But only a few days after I got back to campus, he came over to me, looking a little shy—which on him looked just plain strange—and said, 'Want to go for a pizza or something? My treat.' And so he started using me on a regular basis, in my room when Tony was gone, in his room when his roommate was out. Once I even sucked him off in the men's room at the library, but without the lingerie it wasn't as good. Tony kept fucking my face, too, I guess when he couldn't get laid otherwise, but it was Bret I really wanted. It wasn't because of who he was, really. It wasn't even his looks. It was because of, well, me. I needed him. I wanted to be pretty for him. I wanted to be pretty so someone would love me."

He looked in my eyes with an expression so pure, so vulnerable that it made me ache. It made me want to come. It made me want to screw him.

"Finally, one night, it happened. Tony was spending the night at his latest girlfriend's house, so I invited Bret over. He brought a fifth of Cuervo and a teddy, garters, and stockings. 'I want you to look like a whore,' he said, then took a big gulp from the bottle.

"'A pretty whore,' I told Bret, hardly believing I was saying it. '*Your* pretty whore.'

"Bret took out a condom. 'Don't want to catch anything from some faggot, do I, slut?' he said. I couldn't get words out. I just shook my head. And then he pulled his foreskin back, unrolled the rubber, and lubed up. "Fag, I'm going to fuck you good,' he said. And he did.

"I hadn't been fucked before and it hurt at first, hurt pretty bad when he shoved his way inside me as I lay there on my back, big strong Bret between my stockinged legs. But I managed to take it, threw my arms around him, and his strokes became less brutal. That's when he looked at me blearily and said, 'I love you.' I couldn't believe it. 'I love you, Rick.' Just like that. I felt, well, I felt so damn pretty."

I was beginning to get a more than a little annoyed. I wanted to fuck Rick, just like Bret the frat boy had, but the story obviously meant a lot to him, so I lay there, him in my arms, my fingers up his ass, as he continued.

"That was the only time he said that. In fact, he started to seem more distant; we had sex less frequently. But then it's hard to have a secret affair with someone who's in the same frat house. I can't say I really loved him, not even a little bit. Even then I didn't think so. But I couldn't shake the feeling that I somehow belonged to him, or at least a part of him. Hell, I don't know, maybe I did love him in a way.

"And then one night I was at the pizza place. I overheard some guys a couple of tables over, talking. I really wasn't eavesdropping; they were loudmouths. 'So ever since that girls' underwear stunt, some guys have been calling your house Sigma Queer,' one of them said. And then the reply: 'Dude, it's not the house that's gay. Nobody knows that better than me. It's just this one brother, a guy named Rick. He's nice enough, I suppose, but he's a real big faggot.' I recognized the voice; I didn't even have to turn and see who was talking, though I did look. It was Bret, his back toward me, and the other guys at the table were all laughing and grinning. I ran out in the street, a slice of pepperoni pizza still in my hand.

"A few days later, Bret showed up at my door. I shouldn't have let him in, I guess, but I did. I put on the slip he'd brought. He shoved me down onto the bed, got me on all fours, and pushed the lacy hem up around my waist, and I let him fuck me. I *wanted* him to fuck me, and he used my ass hard. Somewhere in the middle, Tony came back. He sat there watching until Bret shot his load, and then he fucked me, too. After it was over I lay

THE SWEETHEART OF SIGMA QUEER

there in the dark, wanting someone to love me and crying myself to sleep. But that didn't stop me from jacking off the next day when I remembered being fucked by both Tony and Bret.

"Finally, a week or two after that, I kind of realized I'd had enough. I was having a snack in the kitchen of the house when Bret showed up with another frat brother, a senior, a husky dude who always acted real tough. His name, if you can believe it, was Jimbo. He looked at me and said, 'I'm fucking horny and I hear you'll let anybody fuck your ass.' I couldn't stand the guy's attitude. I told him, 'You heard wrong.' 'Bitch,' Bret said. And then Jimbo spat on me, actually spat on me. And that was it. I decided it was time to move out."

And *I* had decided it was time for Rick to put out. Enough. I had let him tell his story, and now my reward was past due. I pushed him back on the bed and climbed on top of him.

"All I wanted was to be pretty," he said.

"You *are* pretty," I said, and I meant it. I ran my hand over his legs, over the black mesh stockings, up to the garter belt. He moaned and spread his legs. My fingers moved to his silky red crotchless panties. My dick was as hard as it gets. I reached over for a rubber.

"You don't have to use that," he said, but I did use it. I didn't want to bring something home, not from a whore like him.

I pushed his legs in the air, my hands against his stockings, his taut muscles beneath. His bigger-than-average dick was stiff against his belly, leaking pre-come. I slapped some lube on his hole, so wet it was soaking his crotchless panties, then positioned my dickhead up against his pussy.

"Pretty," he said. "I want to be pretty for you."

And I slid all the way inside him and started fucking his cunt. His insides felt great, all warm and yielding and wet. I reached under his slip and grabbed one of his little nipples and tweaked it hard. He closed his eyes and licked his lips. Like a slut. Slut. I rammed into his hole, banging him, making him squirm and moan.

"Hurt me with your dick."

"You bet, you little fucking bitch." And I screwed him as hard as I could.

Pretty. He was so pretty. So pretty and fucked up and willing. And good sex, such a good fuck.

Much better than my wife.

TORI'S SECRET

Andrea Miller

B ending down to get the tray out of the cupboard, my dress
rode even farther up my ass and my toes squeezed yet more
painfully into my pointy shoes. Then standing up and opening
the fridge, I noticed different discomforts. In fact, no matter
which way I moved the French maid costume was unbearable.
Tori had given it to me for my birthday the week before, and
when I'd unwrapped it, I had balked. I mean, I was femme, but
this costume crossed a line—and besides, I was tired of presents
from Tori that were really for her. Somehow, though, here I was
in the dinky hat and frilly apron, anyway.

Tori was having friends over to watch a hockey game, and I
could hear them cheering and stomping even with the long hall
separating us. I wished they'd be quieter; it was my name on the
lease, after all. Tori had moved in with me a year before and had
weaseled out of making it official.

I cracked open four beers and placed them on the tray. Then I
reached up and got Tori's favorite glass out of the top cupboard.

She wanted a rum and Coke—a nice tough butch drink to complement the way she could swig it back, the way she could swagger, the way she could pinch my little maid's ass. Boy, did Tori think she was made of metal.

I opened the freezer and grabbed the tray of ice cubes, popped four out, and let them clink to the bottom of the glass. Ice: Now that was something that could spark a good thought about Tori, a memory from the beginning of our relationship. It had been a hot, sticky day, and we'd just gotten back from the beach. "Come here, Kelly," I heard Tori call, but I was in the living room and couldn't tell where her voice was coming from. I walked down the hall and poked my head in the bedroom—no, not there. Then I stepped into the kitchen, and suddenly she was behind me with her arm around my waist and her mouth on my neck, her teeth grazing my skin.

"I'm gonna fuck you so hard and good," she crooned, "that for the rest of your life, when someone rams her fingers into your cunt, you're gonna think of me. You're gonna wish they were my magic fingers inside you." Then in one swift motion she yanked my bikini bottoms down and bent me over the table.

I shut my eyes as Tori wedged her thigh between mine, parting my legs. "Look at that little pucker," she said. "So pink and exposed. Just waiting for some attention. Baby, is this what it needs?"

My asshole felt suddenly like it was on fire, and I tried to wriggle free. Tori had a hand on my back, however, and she was pinning me down. "Relax," she murmured, and as my struggling settled into a slight squirm, I realized that what she was rubbing me with was not hot but rather very cold. Ice cold. And as the ice made contact with my skin, it slowly melted, trickled to my pussy and down my thighs. Christ, it felt good. So slick against the gritty grains of sand left over from the beach that another kind of wetness formed between my legs.

Tori relaxed her hold on my back and bent down—kissed the undersides of my thighs and each globe of my butt cheeks. Then, snaking her warm tongue into my crack, she found my asshole and licked me there until I begged her to make me come.

On a certain level I wish that what followed was nothing special, that when push came to shove Tori couldn't follow through on her cocksure promise to be better with her hands than anyone else. But the truth is, she was that good, and I guess that was the reason I couldn't break it off with her, even though everything about her pissed me off. And I guess that was why she was always so popular with the ladies—even those she hadn't (or rather hadn't yet) fucked. One look at Tori's trimmed nails and strong hands and women instinctively knew she was going to be good.

I topped off the cup with rum, then headed down the hall—my heels falling silently on the carpet all the way to the living room where Tori and her friends were talking.

"There are different kinds of trust," Tori said, looking her friend Katie in the eye. And I thought, fuck, she's getting deeper with Katie than she ever does with me; maybe she occasionally says something real when I'm not around. Tori, after all, hadn't seemed to notice that I'd gotten back from the kitchen.

"It's like this," Tori continued. "You can trust me with your wallet but not with your girlfriend."

Katie visibly bristled, and Tori laughed, punching her arm. "Jesus, man, just kidding." But Katie didn't look comforted, and I definitely wasn't. The thing is, I know about jokes. I know that what makes them funny is that on some level, at least, there's truth in them.

Tori's laughter slowly faded to a giggle—a little butch giggle she probably would've described as a cackle—and everyone else just sat there, looking at the TV or Tori's boots or some other random point. But I don't think any of us really saw anything except a picture of Jacqueline in our minds' eyes. Jacqueline, Katie's girlfriend, with her perfect curves and long dark hair. Jacqueline with her easy smile.

Jacqueline wasn't like the others; Tori didn't just fuck her behind my back. Instead, two months after the hockey game, she left me for her. I knew things hadn't been working out, but finding Tori's note on the coffee table just about killed me. There was my pride thinking, Damn, why didn't I leave her first? There was the eternal pisser that everything always worked out for her, and then there was what made me really raw—that she'd never again bury her fingers in me and then let me suck them off. The force of my reaction, however, went beyond the pain of those three points and crossed into out-of-control. Sobbing and slamming my fists into the walls, I hurtled back to being four years old—to when my father left. I remembered my mother and I coming home to find both his note and the plate he'd used for lunch on the kitchen table. And now, twenty-four years later, that plate seemed a terrible kick in the teeth. After years of marriage, my father couldn't even throw away the crust from his own sandwich.

In a similar way, Tori (in her PS) left me with shit to clean up, too. "I'll be by soon to get my stuff," she wrote. "Maybe you can pack it for me." And sure enough, almost everything Tori owned was still strewn about the apartment. On the closet floor I found one of her T-shirts that smelled like her—like men's deodorant and cigarette smoke. I put it on and crawled into bed, looking for comfort in the cotton. But the clock ticked on without bringing comfort or sleep. Sometimes, forgetting I hated Tori, I'd lodge a pillow next to my belly and remember her sexy, crooked smile and the deep indent her calve muscles created in her shins. At other times, I'd kick off the blankets and plot fantastical schemes for revenge.

Three days later, I called my friend Tracy. "Tori still hasn't come to get her stuff and I doubt she ever will," I said, the telephone cord drooping.

"I could see her doing that," Tracy answered. "She'd think that by not coming, she could avoid conflict."

"But I need her to come, Tracy. I need resolution. I keep thinking I see Tori and Jacqueline everywhere—even on the bus or at the grocery store. I'll never be able to go to Sister's again—somewhere they might actually be."

"You know what?" Tracy asked, and it sounded like she was rapping her nails on a table. "We need to go to Sister's right now because you need to face this. I'll be by your place in an hour."

When I finally left the bar, I wondered what had possessed me to phone Tracy, looking for a shoulder to cry on. She was my best friend, but she didn't know how to be a shoulder. Tracy wanted to fix problems—to take action—and once she had a plan, she was an unstoppable force. "It's Tuesday," she'd assured me. "They won't be there." But Tracy hadn't remembered that there was a drag king show on and that ninety percent of the city's lesbians had bought tickets in advance. So Tori and Jacqueline *were* there—Jacqueline with her hand in Tori's back pocket, her head on Tori's shoulder. Humiliated, I went home before they saw me.

After Tracy left, I wriggled out of my dress and unhooked my bra. Then lifting up my pillow, I found Tori's T-shirt where I'd left it that morning, folded into a neat rectangle. I pulled it over my head as I had every night since finding the note, but this time I couldn't catch her scent—just a whiff of my own perfume, which struck me suddenly as smelling sickly sweet. I decided that in order to sleep I'd need something more of Tori, so I opened the closet. Inside, my half was lined with dresses on hangers trimmed with lace. In Tori's half, the few hangers she had were mostly dangling empty and the bulk of her wardrobe was on the floor with the shoes. I rummaged in her heap until I found her khaki cargo pants. Then, putting them on, I checked myself out in the mirror.

At first, I looked out of the corner of my eye, imagining it was Tori I was seeing. But finally I looked head on and what I saw took me by surprise: I didn't look bad out of a dress. As my build was smaller than Tori's, her clothes hung differently on me, giving me a wiry look that was wolf-sexy and compelled me to complete the outfit.

I found one of Tori's ball caps—a black one—and tucked my blond hair underneath it. I fished her thumb ring out of a bowl of pennies and slipped it on. Then I opened the bottom drawer where she kept her sex toys and dug through the harnesses and dildos. She'd taken the best of them with her, yet I managed to find a nice, thick, black cock and a passable harness. I took off the cargo pants and got the goodies strapped on.

Tori and most of the other women I'd ever dated were stone proud, so it had been a while since I'd worn a cock. But I'd always liked the feel of it, and even now when I had no one to thrust it into, I was getting juicy. I pulled the pants over the silicone and admired the bulge between my legs. Then I lightly ran my fingers over that bulge—my gaze fixed on my refection in the mirror.

Grinding into my hand, I imagined that the cup of my fingers was Tori's cunt, that I was fucking her and that she was loving it—moaning and squirming like a silly bitch. I undid the zipper, letting the dick spring free, and then I dipped a finger into my pussy to slick the head with my own wetness. Chocking the rod, as if doing it hard enough would really make it shoot a load, I felt the rub of the harness working my clit, and I cocked my legs wide open. In the mirror, I watched my nipples poke hard against Tori's T-shirt and watched my hips thrust up and up. I let out one deep moan and came simultaneously with my reflection.

Two nights later, I was decked out in more of Tori's clothes when the doorbell rang. Shit, I thought, I can't answer like this. How could I explain my queer crossdressing to any of my friends, to my mother, or—on the off chance that it was her—to Tori? I stumbled out of the jeans, wallet chain clinking to the ground, and threw on a floral bathrobe. "Hello," I said, opening the door, a little breathless.

Outside was Katie, running her fingers through her short, sandy hair. "I've been wanting to talk to you," she said. "But I wasn't sure you'd want to…"

I was surprised Katie had come, because she'd always been more Tori's friend than mine—she and Jacqueline had just been people I'd see at parties or events. But Katie had nothing to worry about. I was very glad to see her; finally, I'd have someone to talk to about the breakup, someone who wouldn't get sick of hearing about it. I invited her in, and we settled into the living room, with her on the sofa and me in the armchair. "I don't get it," she began. "Things were fine between Jacqueline and me, but it's like women can't resist Tori."

"Tell me about it," I said. "It doesn't matter what a woman thinks her type is—she'll fall for Tori, anyway."

"Yeah, Jacqueline likes butch blondes like her, but she usually goes for someone not built quite so much like a brick shit house. You know, someone kind of wiry like me."

The two of us went quiet for a minute—a real tear-in-the-beer bout of silence. "Katie," I finally said. "I'm being a crap hostess. Do you want a drink?"

"What've you got?" she answered, following me to the kitchen. I looked in the fridge. Tori's pop had all gone flat, but two of her beers were left. Cracking them open, I handed one to Katie and noticed she was looking down. Following her gaze, I realized my robe was sliding open, revealing the curve of my breast. I quickly adjusted it and Katie laughed. Still smiling, she pulled me to her, kissing me. Her lips and tongue were hesitant but precise, and I felt so lonely with Tori gone that for a moment I melted into Katie. It didn't feel right, though. I knew I was being pathetic—making out with Tori's leftovers.

"I can't do this," I said, crying. "I'm not ready."

Breakups spur change. You know, people do stuff like cut their hair or move across the country. Me? I wanted to change jobs. After doing three years at university, I'd dropped out and gotten work at an art gallery. Still there seven years later, it was wearing thin with the same shit daily. Yuppies buying Inuit art. Yuppies buying abstract art. Yuppies buying something a little daring.

About a week after Katie's visit, I was once again scanning the classifieds for a new position. As usual, there wasn't much unless you aspired to be a babysitter, but finally in the right-hand corner I spotted it—a want ad for an assistant manager at Between the Lines bookstore. The very same shop where Jacqueline worked.

For a moment, I just sat there grinning with my coffee growing cold. Then I jumped up to find Katie's number. I had a lot of things to do. I had the perfect revenge to execute.

The following evening I showed my hairdresser a picture of a seventeen-year-old skater boy and said I wanted his hair. My hairdresser, who had for years known me and my femme ways, clutched at my long locks—drama queen shock written on his face. "I'm serious," I said. I *was* serious. I'd spent hours milking Katie for information on Jacqueline's turn-ons, and now I intended to live up to all of them—including the short hair.

Not wanting Katie to know what I was up to, it had been complicated getting information out of her. I'd had to pretend I wanted to know intimate details because I was nursing an obsessive jealousy for Jacqueline and, as a kind of give and take, I'd had to dole out similar information about Tori. Ultimately though, the trouble I'd taken had been worth it. I now knew, for example, that Tori was not the ideal lover for Jacqueline as Jacqueline liked both getting fucked and fucking. I knew there was no way Tori would let Jacqueline strap it on or let her slip a finger in, but *I* was more than ready to play those games. To do anything, really.

Just about finished, the hairdresser's razor hummed against my neck and his scissors snipped at a few rogue strands. I looked at my hair lying in clumps on the tiled floor. Then I looked in the mirror and sucked my teeth. Fuck, I wanted to blow a kiss to that sexy butch looking back at me. This was going to work. All I had to do was get the job and buy the cologne Jacqueline loved—the one Katie couldn't stand and had always refused to wear.

Two weeks later, it was my first day at Between the Lines and the manager was showing me the ropes—giving me the grand tour, introducing me to the staff. Everything was going well, but I was nervous knowing that Jacqueline could be anywhere and that at any moment she could spring out like a pop-up monster in a children's book. As chance would have it, however, I'd had nothing to worry about—it was I who popped out at her. The manager and I rounded the magazine rack and then there she was, kneeling in front of the Philosophy section with her back to us. "Jacqueline," the manager said, clearing his throat. "I'd like to introduce you to Kelly."

From her place on the floor, Jacqueline slowly looked up at me—her easy smile first playing over my boots and then up and up until she met my eyes and the happy curve of her lips was lopped off. Sliced up by three huge shocks. One, we were face to face for the first time since she'd stolen my girlfriend. Two, henceforth she'd have to deal with me daily. And three, I didn't look like she remembered.

Fortunately, by this point, so many people had expressed shock over my new look that I'd learned (at least) to shrug that off. Tracy, for instance, had told me such quick comfort in a 180-degree turn meant I didn't know my true identity—a bullshit line, I concluded, to conceal her own fear. The very human fear of gray. Of worlds colliding. Of categories blurring. Yes, people want tidy distinctions. Butch or femme. Hot or cold. Love or hate. Villain or victim. And so it was making people very nervous to see me with short hair. To hear me say I'd always had butch and femme sides and that the butch had just been waiting to learn how to swagger.

As I said, though, Jacqueline's look of bewilderment had various sources—not just the butch thing—and so it was a zillion times harder for her than for others. That's what I was thinking, anyway, when the book she'd been trying to shelve slipped from her fingers and fell to the floor with a thud.

The manager's gaze flicked a triangle from me to Jacqueline to the book. Pages spread. Spine arched. "Have you met before?" he asked.

Jacqueline avoided me for weeks, but it wasn't wasted time. I was studying her and our game by spending a few minutes of every shift in the Hunting and Fishing section. I'd open a random book to a random page and I'd read until I found some nugget of advice I needed, and in that way I learned how to circle in slowly, how to interpret every gesture, the tilt of her head, the flick of her hair. And I learned when to start reeling in.

"Jacqueline," I said one afternoon when all the signs were right and we were alone in the staff room. "We should talk." She had a peach in one hand and a book in the other; instead of putting them down, she gripped them tighter, apparently not noticing the trail of peach juice that dripped down her fingers and all the way to her wrist. I licked my lips and sat down across from her.

"You obviously aren't comfortable around me," I began. "But I'm not at all mad at you."

"No?" she said, her voice lifted in hope.

"No—you did me a favor. Things weren't working between Tori and me. I couldn't be myself with her... The two of you, on the other hand, you make sense together."

Afraid of sounding smarmy, I paused then and looked at Jacqueline, trying to read her. The corners of her lips were beginning to curl up into their natural position, and her blue eyes were so wide open the fringes of her lashes were forced vertical. She'd put down her book and fruit, and she now seemed on the verge of clasping her hands together. Yes, she was buying it. Of course she was, I thought, gaining confidence. She wanted nothing more than to have her guilty conscience soothed.

We talked until the microwave clock said 1:28 and I reminded that her we had better get back to work. "But let's have a hug first," I said when we were both standing.

Without hesitation, Jacqueline threw her arms around my

neck, showing me how everything about her was deliciously soft—the crush of her breasts against mine, the tickle of her angora sweater, even the fuzzy smell of peaches on her fingers. I realized I was going to enjoy fucking her for more than just the ironic revenge of it, and in the same instant she realized she was attracted to me. I could tell by of the way she instinctively touched the back of my neck then quickly stiffened.

I don't know what it was Jacqueline liked about me—the hair, the cologne, the lean press of my bones, or something else altogether. Maybe something perverse like curiosity of where her lover had been. All I know is that hug marked the beginning of months of seduction. Months of standing too close, of double entendre, of private jokes. I remember once being inches away from her in the storeroom. Hemmed in by books— yes—though mostly that close just because we wanted to be. Jacqueline had her face turned up to me and her lips parted, ready to be kissed. I leaned in like I was going to oblige her and then I quickly turned away. My mouth was watering for her, too, but I knew it was better this way. To make her wait until wanting crushed her guilt, made her reckless. And it was another month before she was that hopelessly ensnared and an opportunity arose—dished up in fact by Tori, who forgot to pick her up one night.

"Jacqueline, it's dark and wet out there," I said. "Let me drive you home."

The streetlight in front of their apartment cast a weird orange glow over everything in the car, while their living room window was a perfect black rectangle with no one home. I locked all the doors with the press of a button, turned off the ignition, and let my thigh brush hers. "You aren't going anywhere," I said, jingling the keys, flashing my best demonic smile.

She playfully grabbed for the keys, but I whisked them behind my back. Then she flung her arms around my waist, pressing into me, and continued trying to snatch them. Now her face was inches from mine and I couldn't resist. Loving the risk of it, the possibility of Tori showing up at any minute, I leaned in and kissed her—a sweet, soft kiss that left me wanting more bite. I pulled away and handed her the cold metal teeth. "I can't believe you fell for that," I sneered. "It's the oldest trick in the school yard."

Jacqueline face fogged into bewildered, then darkened into pissed off—just what we needed for something more savage. We kissed again and this time began humping with the urgency of dogs, so hard I thought her slit would strip me of my skin, grind down my bones. I wanted to hurt her, I wanted to make her come, and I no longer knew the line between those extremes. I jacked up her skirt and drove my fingers in.

Her cunt was slick yet it clamped onto my knuckles with the strength of a snake crushing a mouse in its guts. I rammed harder, slithering to my knees between the dashboard and the passenger seat. Flicked my tongue on her clit—once, twice, thrice. Felt her shudder and pound her fist into my back. Then I pulled away. Looked down at her shaved pussy—a cleft moon in the night.

"Let's go to your place," she said, her voice throaty like I'd never heard it before.

After that, Jacqueline and I fucked everywhere: in my car like the hard line of the seats didn't exist, like we couldn't ride too fast; in my bed with all the nasty irony of using Tori's cocks; and even in the store—in the staff bathroom during breaks and between the shelves after hours.

Jacqueline talked about leaving Tori for me, but wanting more, I put her off. I wanted Tori to catch us, to see for myself the smugness wiped from her face. So I left hints—the whisper of teeth marks on Jacqueline's skin, for example—hoping something would raise her suspicions and make her spy on Jacqueline. Months passed and the lies became more complicated.

"Tori went to her mum's," Jacqueline said one Friday night in the car. "She asked me to go, but I said I couldn't. I said I should visit my folks, too."

"Are you going to?"

"Of course not. I wouldn't miss the chance to be with you all weekend."

Excellent, I thought, taking a sudden turn that veered us away from my apartment, our original destination. At the very least this would be an opportunity to leave more clues—my hair in their bed, my scent on their towels. And at best this would be the climax of it all and we would finally get caught.

"Where are you going?" Jacqueline asked, looking nervous but not saying no.

Their apartment was new—the walls brilliantly white, the carpet pink like the inside of a shell. Floral sofa, books lining shelves, soft light. Those were Jacqueline's touches. Of Tori I could see gum wrappers on the table, clothes slumped on the floor, dirty dishes in the sink. No, I decided, I didn't miss Tori.

Jacqueline leaned down to undo her sandals, and I admired her ass—two firm, fine grapefruits I couldn't help but touch. Still bending over, Jacqueline wriggled against my hand, giving me access to everything. She was wearing red capris, and through the cloth her pussy felt like a squishy bun fresh from the oven. I undid the button, then the zipper, then pulled the pants down to her ankles. Pulled down her white panties sprinkled with hearts. And all the while I thought about how Jacqueline and Tori surely must have fucked in this same spot.

Jacqueline stood up and pulled off her shirt. "Now you," she said, undoing all my buttons one by one. When we were both naked, her fingers trickled over my skin. My nipples turned into hard pebbles, my cunt into a river. We tumbled to the floor. Jacqueline swept her hands over my thighs, belly, breasts. Broad strokes that finally condensed into tiny wet circles playing my clit. She slipped a finger inside and, just as Tori predicted, I thought of her. But not like she said I would. No, I was imagining her walking in, watching. Maybe looking crushed or maybe jacking off to the rhythm of Jacqueline sliding in and out—two different yet delicious images that made my hips rock faster. Yes, my fantasies were so real I could hear Tori's footsteps, the key in the lock, the door swinging open.

Then Jacqueline froze suddenly and I realized fantasy and reality had finally merged. Tori, with her hand still on the doorknob, was standing above us with her mouth gaping open. I tried not to grin, yet for those first few seconds victory felt sexier than the orgasm I'd missed out on. Then, however, I noticed something was off—not as I'd imagined it. Tori looked neither turned on nor crushed, but rather a mixture of the two and then some. Her face contained traces of things that seemed to have no origin—guilt and amusement, even. But of course there was an origin, and she soon bounded in on Tori's heels, not noticing until it was too late that Jacqueline and I were on the floor.

"I love it when you fuck me up the ass," Katie declared to Tori.

LIKE A GIRL

Alison Tyler

Show me what you've got."

I hesitated, unsure.

"Show me, Ivy."

I was standing there, in indigo jeans, tight, white T-shirt, and green army jacket. My hair was slicked back off my face, and all of my jewelry was off. I don't have much in the chest department, but what I do have was pressed flat by two separate athletic bras. Here was my thrift-store attempt to dress as a man. That, and the harness and dildo trapped under my Levi's.

"Drop your trousers and show me."

I worked the belt, pulled the buttons on my fly, and then lowered my jeans. The cock, which had been molded up against my flat belly, now sprang forward.

Logan laughed at the sight. I hadn't wanted something realistic. The veiny ones had given me the creeps. But this was beautiful. Midnight blue with swirls of white. Big but not too big. I slid my hand along the shaft and Logan stopped laughing.

"You touch yourself like a girl." There was both disgust and pity in his tone.

"I *am* a girl."

"Not in that outfit. You're trying for Officer Joe or something, right? Fresh out of basic training. Yet you grip your joint in that wimpy manner. 'Oooh, look at me! I have a cock.' Christ, it's not even a cock. It's some girly toy." He'd nailed me. He was right. I had gone half the distance in my efforts, hadn't been willing to go the full route.

"Try again." His voice was cold. The rules of the games had changed.

I thought of what Logan looked like when he came on me, standing next to the bed, working his hand on his own cock. I found that vision mesmerizing, his hand, jerking faster and faster, touching himself harder and with more power than I'd ever dare.

With difficulty, I tried to channel that sexy image, tried to climb inside. I closed my eyes and let my head go back, feeling a little more powerful in my Docs than I would have barefoot, despite the fact that my jeans were pooled around my ankles, limiting my mobility. Concentrating, I slid my hand along the smooth plastic cock. Up and down, squeezing hard, speeding up.

"Spit on your palm," Logan whispered.

I did. Or I tried. Waiting for the inevitable "You spit like a girl" comment to come. I could easily have licked my palm. I could have unbuckled the toy and deep-throated it with finesse. But this was different. Suddenly, this had become a lesson—work rather than play.

"Jesus," Logan said, and I opened my eyes, watching as he stood up from the sofa and came to my side. He pushed me hard back up against the wall, spit cleanly into his own palm and started to work my cock for me. And in an instant, I felt as

if it really *were* my cock, as if I truly had become connected to
this toy—or as if I were in an X-rated version of the children's
classic fable of the *Velveteen Rabbit* and the synthetic cock had
somehow turned real.

Logan's ice-blue eyes burned into mine as he stroked me, forcing the connection between the two of us. And I could imagine
us somewhere else. In the back room of a club, Logan manhan-
dling me. Others watching. An audience forming because of our
heat. Or out behind some bar, in the parking lot, Logan using his
own spit to lube me up, knowing that in seconds he was going to
have to stand aside, to watch me shoot my come on the dirt.

And then another image, one that made my heart seem to
still. Logan doing this. Exactly this. To Caleb. And right then, as
I stared at Logan, wondering if he could see the questions swirling in my eyes, the front door opened and in walked Cal.

My breath caught. Each time Logan's hand pumped my cock,
he pressed the base of the toy back against my clit. And each time
I felt that connection, I thought I would climax. He didn't stop.
He didn't turn or say a word. He kept going, pausing only to add
a bit more spit to his palm, so that I felt he was greasing me.

Caleb froze. I'm sure something flippant was on the tip of
his tongue, but maybe he caught a look on Logan's face and
that stopped him. He was able to shut the door behind him,
and then he stood totally still, and I knew he was waiting for
instructions.

"You're going to come for me, boy?" Logan murmured,
crooning to me but teasing somehow. Taunting me for dressing
like this in the first place. He'd told me to buy an outfit for Cal.
He hadn't told me to dress up myself.

"Yes, sir."

"Then come."

My knees would have buckled if Logan hadn't used one hand

to pin my shoulder against the wall, holding me in place easily as the shudders worked through me. The orgasm was almost frighteningly intense. Embarrassingly so, as I was being watched fiercely by the two men in my life. And then it was over, and Logan let me go, and I hiked up my jeans and sank down to the floor, letting the wall support me now.

"You even come like a girl," Logan said as he poured himself a fresh drink.

I didn't answer that. I didn't have anything to say.

Logan didn't give any instructions to Caleb. Cal just came forward, grabbed me up in his arms, and whispered to me that I was so fucking sexy. "Didn't think you could look like that," he said, eyes roaming over my outfit. "You're such a girly girl usually."

And he was right. I am. But on this night, I was something else. Logan motioned to Caleb, and he nodded, grabbing my hand, pulling me back to the bedroom. Logan didn't follow, and I understood that I was the one who was going to have to explain the next part of the scenario to Logan's right-hand man. At least, I thought I was. But as soon as Caleb saw the purchases spread out on the bed, he seemed to understand.

"You know where he sent me today?"

I shook my head.

"To a salon," he hesitated, and then: "For a wax job."

I watched as Cal peeled off his clothes, revealing the smooth expanse of his chest. He had also very recently shaved his face, not relying on the morning's visit with the razor. I sat on the edge of the bed, surprised at how quickly, how willingly, he got naked. Had Logan prepped him? Or was Caleb just such an obedient assistant that he would do whatever Logan requested of him. Even when that request wasn't verbally given.

"What's next?" he said, staring now at me.

I offered over the panties, and his cheeks turned slightly pink as he pulled them on. "You had to get ruffles," he said softly.

"They were specially requested," I told him.

Caleb nodded, waiting for me to pass over the white pinafore, like something from *Alice in Wonderland*. Or something from an acid dream. A pinafore with ruffles, as well, but one in a size that would fit the well-built man standing feet from me. He pulled the dress over his head and then gave me a mock curtsey. I started to giggle.

"You think I'm pretty?" he teased.

"No. Not really."

He looked hurt. "Well, why the fuck not?"

"You're not done." I handed him the wig, and he took it and stood in front of the dresser, adjusting the wig over his short blond hair. He was looking more like a large doll at this point than a man in girl's clothing or an actual girl. But I hadn't gotten the feeling that Logan wanted Caleb to look like a girl. He seemed to be making a point. Showing Caleb what he could make him do. And Caleb was willingly playing along. It would take far greater skill than what I possessed to make Caleb look passably female.

When he had the wig in place, I came to his side and did the makeup, going for a lighter version of Tim Curry in *Rocky Horror*. No whiteface, but plenty of smudged eye shadow, dark lipstick, rouge. Then I took a step back and admired the outfit.

"Oh, wait," I told him. "Shoes!"

I'd gotten the two pairs, but realized suddenly that I'd forgotten nylons. Quickly, I rummaged around through my drawer. He'd never fit into my pantyhose, but he easily slid on a pair of stockings, ones that had a self-sticking band at the top—rendering garters unnecessary. Once he'd slid the stockings over his silky-smooth legs—he'd had the full wax job here, as well, I noted—I offered him the choice of heels. To my surprise, he chose the superhigh ones, and he walked gracefully in them, making me wonder if perhaps this wasn't Caleb's first time in drag.

"Now what?" he asked, gazing at his own reflection.

"I guess I bring you back down the hall to Logan."

"He didn't say what he was going to do?"

I shook my head.

"Did he dress you himself?"

"No," I told him. "I was inspired by what I'd bought for you."

But before we could return to Logan, the bedroom door opened and he entered the room. He took a moment to drink in the brand-new Caleb, before sitting down on the chair in the corner. He still had a whiskey glass in hand, and from the look in his eye, he seemed to be waiting for a performance to start. But Caleb and I were like marionettes without their puppeteer. We had no idea what to do next.

"You're pretty like that," Logan said finally, and I saw Caleb's cheeks turn even pinker beneath the cotton-candy wash of blush I'd given them. "Very feminine. Although not quite female. A perfect partner for Ivy, who has stepped into the masculine role tonight, without managing to look all the way like a boy."

He took a sip of his drink and continued to stare for a moment before saying, "It's been a brutal few weeks for me, and I was looking for something different tonight. Something unusual. I don't know exactly how this idea came to mind. Maybe I took one too many drives past the windows of Dream Dresser. Or maybe I've always wondered what Ivy would look like in the driver's seat." He was thinking aloud. That's how it seemed to me, and Caleb and I remained silent, his audience, his tiny cast.

"Kiss her, Ivy," he said suddenly, and I realized he wanted me to kiss Caleb, and that Caleb was—for the moment—"her."

I did so automatically, stepping forward, cradling Caleb's face in my hands, kissing his mouth. Not able to think of him as a woman but easily able to be turned on by the gloss of his lipstick smearing to my own mouth.

"No, not like that," Logan sighed. "Kiss her like you like to be kissed. Kiss her the way I kiss you."

My mind whirled, but I thought I understood. I gripped the back of Caleb's neck, taking charge, pulling him forcefully toward me, and I kissed him fiercely, the one in power, the one making the rules. I bit his bottom lip when we parted and felt Caleb shudder slightly at that tiny, insignificant spark of pain.

"Better," Logan said softly. "Much better."

And then we were waiting again, standing there in front of him, two actors before the director, or two naughty juveniles before the headmaster, waiting for the next command—the next direction—the next...

"Spread her out on the bed. Make her feel wanted."

Crazy stuff, this. But, of course, I didn't argue. Instead, I gently led Caleb to the bed, and he willingly lay down on his back, looking up at me. I saw trust in his eyes and that made me feel suddenly scared. He had faith in me. Faith I didn't have in myself. But when I continued to meet his gaze, I felt a bit of power transfer from Caleb to me, and I knew what to do next. If I were Logan, I'd be binding this pretty doll's wrists over her head. And so I did, without a command from my man, without a word of instruction, taking Caleb's wrists and cuffing them easily, then looping the chain over the hook above our bed. Logan chuckled at this little bit of improvisation, and I could tell he approved.

I could tell Caleb approved as well, because his pinafore had become a pup tent. The towering white dress turned me on instantly, gave me more confidence than I'd had all evening. I almost felt my own cock twitch in response.

.

With Caleb captured so, I waited for Logan's next word, but when I looked at him, he simply winked at me and nodded. So I understood that he liked the direction I was taking. I was on my own now—at least for the moment—I had to be creative. And I had to be in charge.

But what did that mean exactly? I thought for a moment, considered what I most wanted to do. My eyes returned to the pup-tented pinafore and quickly I knew. I slid on the bed between Caleb's legs and lifted the dress. Caleb's eyes were on me. Focused. Intent. I easily slid his panties down his thighs, pulling them all the way off, even over the skyscraper heels, and then I crawled back to my spot, regarding Caleb's massive hard-on for only a second before dipping my head down to taste...

Caleb groaned darkly as my mouth welcomed his cock. He arched his hips and pulled on the chains that bound his wrists, tugged with a shocking intensity, even though I knew he didn't want to get away. I licked around the tip of his cock, then bobbed my head, taking more of him inside my mouth with each passing second.

Yes, I was turned on by the whole scenario, but mostly because of Logan watching. The fact that Caleb was dressed as a doll didn't make me wet. It was being in charge, feeling the harness and silicone toy still in place under my jeans, and knowing precisely what I was going to be doing with them before the night was over.

Logan sipped his drink. I could feel him watching me. I could feel his intense blue eyes wandering over my body, taking in every motion. I performed for him, licking Caleb like a kitty, working to make his whole cock disappear down my throat. I was lost in this world, shimmying my hips, tossing my hair out of my face when a strand managed to escape the gel and fall forward, until suddenly Logan's hand was on the back of my neck, gripping me up at the nape like a mama cat grabs her kittens. Momentarily stunned, my body tensed and I had to work to meet Logan's eyes.

"You suck cock like a girl, too," he said softly. Yet however cold his tone was, I realized he was right. I might be wearing the strap-on dick. I might be dressed—to the best of my abilities—like a boy toy, like one of those hunky young men for hire out on the Strip. But I was a girl. Heart and soul of a girl. Hungry mouth of a girl. Logan had my body frozen in his strong grip, and I felt as if I wouldn't be able to breathe again until he gave permission.

"You're trying to turn me on," Logan said. "You think you're starring in some porno film, with all your hair flicking and your overacting."

He'd nailed me, yet I didn't know what he wanted, didn't know why he was chastising me.

"Like this," he said, shocking me with the rough way he pushed me aside, so that I fell back on the mattress, tripped by Caleb's thigh, coming to rest on the far side of the bed. Logan gripped Caleb's shaft, his fist firm, and he jerked the boy's cock, using my own spit as lube. Caleb looked as if he were going to pass out. The mix of his current pleasure and the fear of impending pain were vying for first place in his eyes.

Logan worked Caleb with finesse. Fast and furiously, his fist pumping on Caleb's cock, his face, when I dared to look up at it, intent, as if he were on a mission. There was a dangerous look in his eyes that made me quiver. Somehow, I knew right then what was going to happen next. What this whole night was ultimately about. Somehow, I understood and I felt as if the world had stopped.

No, that's not right. I felt as if my world had shattered.

As if he were playing with his own cock, as if he were the

one being jerked off, Logan seemed to gauge Caleb's limits to perfection. Right before the boy came, Logan bent down and took Cal's cock in his mouth. He sucked him hard, differently than I had. He sucked him like a man who knew his way around a cock. Cal arched his hips and came powerfully, and Logan didn't miss a drop.

I stayed where I was, watching the two. Watching the connection between them. A connection I realized I'd never have. I stayed where I was, as the tears started to streak down my face, as Logan turned Cal over, preparing to fuck him.

I stayed where I was, in spite of the silent sobs, in spite of the way my body shook so hard that my teeth chattered. And I cried like a girl. Because beneath the drag, and under the toy cock, and in spite of Logan's instructions, it's all I could ever be.

MICHELLE, MA BELLE

Marcy Sheiner

Many years ago, before I knew what a transvestite was—
I had a vague notion it had something to do with a
sex change—and before I'd explored the far reaches of gender-
bending, I inadvertently stumbled into a relationship with a
crossdressing man.

Michael and I had been going out for several months and had
become fairly open about our sexual fantasies. But it took nearly
a year before he revealed his biggest secret—the contents of his
bottom dresser drawer. He was terrified of being ridiculed, but
my reaction was mostly envy: I fairly drooled over his collection of expensive camisoles, garter belts, push-up bras, and lacy
stockings. Relieved, he told me that for years he'd been dressing
up in secret, sometimes calling a phone-sex service to describe
his outfits, asking the operator to treat him like a woman.

This was fascinating stuff to me. Since I'm bisexual, the
notion of my man dressed as a woman excited me. But it
turned out that though Michael had all the right accoutrements

of femininity, he was a total klutz when it came to hair and makeup. He wanted me to teach him how to look ultrafemme.

The next night I brought over a long blond wig and a small suitcase full of makeup and perfume. I felt like a little girl again, about to dress up my dolls. First, I shaved his legs, underarms, and chest—a messy task, since Michael was quite hairy. Then, I rubbed scented oil all over him, massaging it into his skin as he sighed with pleasure. I put a pair of red bikini panties on him, loving the incongruous sight of the bulge through the silky crotch. Next, I put on a red strapless bra that hooked in front, well-padded so it stayed up and gave him the illusion of breasts. I snapped on a black garter belt studded with little red hearts, holding up black lacy stockings. I slid his feet into a pair of hot-pink six-inch heels.

Dressed in these undergarments, Michael sat in front of the mirror while I did his makeup. I powdered and rouged his cheeks, glued on fake eyelashes, and drew shadows on his lids. For extra effect, I gave him a beauty mark right beside his lips, which were outlined in ruby-red lipstick. Then I applied fake fingernails, painting them to match his mouth. All the while he was staring into the mirror, awed by his transformation. The pièce de résistance was the wig, which I combed a dozen different ways until we agreed he looked best with it swept sideways over one eye. He stood, put on a tight, hot-pink satin dress with a bow at the line of cleavage, and sashayed around the room for my inspection.

I was dazzled by the fantasy girl I'd created. Not only was I proud of my handiwork, I was downright envious—Michael was far more gorgeous as a woman than I. Not even his rippling biceps detracted from his femininity; they just added erotic mystery.

We hadn't planned to go out, but it seemed a shame to keep

Michael hidden away. I spent an inordinate amount of time getting myself ready, until finally Michael said cutely, "Don't try to compete, honey, you'll never win."

Giggling like girlfriends, we stepped out into the night. Heads turned as we strode through the city streets and into a small nightclub. The maître d' totally ignored me as he ogled Michael and gave us the best seats in the house. We drank wine and looked at one another, our eyes twinkling with our shared secret. Suddenly, I heard a male voice call my name. I turned to see an old friend, Jack, heading toward our table.

"Hey, Denise, long time, no see. How's it going?" His eyes slid over to check out my girlfriend.

"Fine, I'm good," I said. "Um, Jack, this is Mi-Michelle," I stammered.

"Pleased to meet you," said Jack, staring openly at Michael's fake bosom. "Mind if I join you girls?"

Before I could answer, Jack pulled up a chair and proceeded to spend the next two hours fawning over "Michelle"—buying her drinks, asking about her life and work, even letting his hand brush across her thigh once or twice. To my utter amazement, Michael responded just like a woman. He spoke in a higher than normal pitch, batted his fake eyelashes, acted coy and charming. I began to wonder if I'd created a monster: Michael seemed totally convinced that he was indeed "Michelle." What if he waltzed off with Jack, forgetting the shock he'd deliver once undressed?

At the end of the evening, Jack asked Michelle for her phone number. To my vast relief, Michael told him, with infinite finesse, that although he'd enjoyed Jack's company, he was in a monogamous relationship.

At home, Michael continued to play the femme. I was on fire, looking forward to ravishing my gorgeous woman. She lay down on the bed, propped herself on one arm, and said seductively, "Gee, Denise, I hope you're not angry with me for flirting with Jack."

"I'm not angry," I said, taking off my clothes. "But you do know that you're mine, Michelle. I created you."

I lay down next to her and took her arms in my hands and pinned them over her head, while my leg pushed her skirt up, forcing her thighs apart. Michelle sighed demurely.

I ran my hand up and down her legs, over the silky stockings. Then I reached back, tugged at her zipper, and removed her dress. I lay on top of her and cupped her "breasts" together, kissing her neck, her ears, her scented throat. She moaned and thrashed her head from side to side as I made my way down her belly to the silk panties. With one fierce movement I ripped them off, tearing them in half. Michael gasped as I took his cock in my hand and squeezed.

I sat back a moment to look at him/her. S/he now wore only the bra, garter belt, and stockings, and his fat cock throbbed expectantly. Her heavily made-up eyes gazed at me, a look of pleading swimming in their blue pools.

"Take me," s/he whispered.

I climbed on top and straddled his cock, squeezing gently as I nudged it into my dripping pussy. "Spread your legs, cunt," I whispered. "I'm gonna fuck you like you've never been fucked before."

She groaned as I began to move rhythmically up and down on his cock, my legs in between his. That cock no longer felt like a part of Michael's body; it was mine. I was the one with the cock, fucking my woman's pussy.

"Yes, oh, yes," she moaned, closing her eyes in delirium. I leaned down and kissed her lipsticked mouth hard, thrusting my tongue down her throat. I pulled her hair, holding her head back, while grinding my pelvis, burying his cock deeper inside me. It throbbed and stiffened, and I knew he was about to come. I let my own orgasm wash over me then; it felt as if I were the one shooting my load into him/her. When our orgasms subsided, I lay my cheek against his and was stunned to feel tears. Questioningly, I looked at Michael/Michelle.

"I've wanted this all my life," he sobbed. "Do you think I'm a pervert?"

I kissed him lovingly. "No, sweetie, I don't think you're a pervert." I looked at his vulnerable, open face. His femme image was disintegrating as mascara ran down his cheeks, leaving gooey black streaks. "But there is one aspect of being female you've yet to master."

"What's that?" he asked.

"Never, never cry until after you've removed your makeup."

BEEFEATER

Lisabet Sarai

Y ou know what I want." I can barely get the words out between gasps. Phil's got my blouse unbuttoned and is diligent-
ly sucking my nipple, with the expected effect. He stops briefly
to swirl his tongue in a deft circle around the aching nub, then
nips at the tip. I moan as my clit jumps in sympathy.

Encouraged, he fastens his mouth on mine while he sneaks
his hand up my thigh. I'm sopping and dying for him to touch
me, but I slap his hand away.

"No way! You're not getting into my knickers until you
agree."

"Oh, come on, Moe. You know I can't do it."

"Of course you can. If you want to. If you want me—want
me enough." He bends to my breasts for another long, delicious
suckle. He's trying to soften me up. I mustn't let him know how
much success he's having.

"Really, I can't. It's like—sacrilege." There's genuine distress
on his face, but it might just be the result of frustrated lust.

"Those uniforms were designed by Queen Victoria, for Christ's sake."

I snuggle up to him with a sweet smile. "I know. That's part of what makes it so hot. The centuries of tradition. Don't you think that it would be hot, Phil?" I stroke his swollen cock through his jeans and give him a wet kiss with lots of tongue. It's hardly possible, but I feel him become bigger and harder. "It's not like this is just for me. I know you'll enjoy it."

"Yeah, but if Geoff catches me, I'm finished. A halberd through the heart! You know how he is about the Warders."

"He won't, I promise. We'll be extra careful. We'll do it when he's on duty."

"And what about my mum?"

"Doesn't she play bridge a couple of nights a week?"

"On Tuesdays and Thursdays, most weeks."

"So all you need to do is figure out the next Tuesday or Thursday night that Geoff's on the watch." I find the bulb of his cock and pinch it through the denim. He yelps. "Should be easy for a smart guy like you."

"Okay, okay, you win. Tell me the details of your devious scheme, and I'll do what I can." Phil stands up and starts pacing back and forth in front of the TV. He's trying to get his hard-on to subside. Mum's due back from work any minute, so I've got to talk fast.

I lay out my plan. As I do, I get wetter and wetter. I've dreamed about this since I was in my preteens. Maybe earlier. But until Uncle Geoff, the man we all thought was a confirmed bachelor, married Aunt Helen, I never saw a chance to turn my fantasy into reality.

I remember sitting on Uncle Geoff's lap when I was really young, four or five. It was a vast expanse of navy blue, with lovely red highlights. Geoff liked to show off his uniform when he came over to visit us. And he did look fine in it. He's not tall, but he's solid, and his sandy hair and beard look golden showing against the rich, dark blue of his hat brim.

Even now, I remember the feel of the tight-woven wool against my thighs. It was smooth, almost silky, not scratchy like the wool skirt and blazer my mum made me wear to church in the winter. I can bring back the scent, too—smoky cigarettes and wood fires, with just a hint of my uncle's Old Spice aftershave.

By the time I was old enough to be getting myself off, my mind was full of men in archaic blue-and-red costumes, touching me as I touched myself. They were faceless but unflaggingly eager.

Some folks, I know, will start quoting Freud to me at this point, babbling on about father figures and displacement and the subconscious. It's true that I don't remember my dad, that Uncle Geoff was all the father I had. But I didn't lust after my uncle. Just his uniform.

I had a normal sex life. I lost my virginity in the last year of sixth form, then shagged a couple of guys during my two years at college. They didn't know that when I came, I was imagining blue wool and garnet trim. At first, I mentally dressed them in the Beefeater uniform. After a while, though, I realized that I got more turned on picturing myself in the Yeoman Warders' costume.

Anyway, it was all just fantasy until last summer.

As soon as I met my cousin Phil at Geoff and Helen's wedding, I knew that he fancied me. And to be honest, the feeling was mutual. I didn't let on, though. I figured I could use the attraction to get his help.

Phil is artistically pale, with messy black hair, green eyes, and a cynical grin. He looks just like the devil that he is. He actually hit on me at the wedding reception, cornering me and feeling me up in the coatroom. Here at last was the accomplice that I needed. He was clever, too, working on his MBA at Imperial College.

He turned out to be more timid than I expected. I had to work hard to convince him that some ancient English god would not strike him down with a bolt of lightning for conspiring with me. Lust, however, is a powerful motivator.

"Maureen, I'm home." Mum bustles into the den only ten minutes after Phil leaves, juggling sacks of groceries.

"Here, let me help." I take two of the bags and follow her into the kitchen. Mum considers me to be something of a disappointment, twenty-four and still living at home, working as a shopgirl when Andy's already a junior partner in accountancy and Cassie has given her two grandkids. But the truth is she'd be awfully lonely if I took off, too. Of course, I will someday. But at the moment, my goals are more near term.

"How was work?" she asks, putting the potatoes on to boil.

"Slow. Lucy sent me home early, since they didn't need me." Of course, I don't mention that Phil picked me up from work in his cute green Mini, or our clinch in the den.

"You really should look for something more challenging, Maureen. Something with more of a future."

"Yes, you're right, Mum." I'm saved by the sound of my mobile ringing. I stroll off to the den to have some privacy.

"Tomorrow."

"Tomorrow?" I mentally check the calendar. Tomorrow is in fact Thursday.

"Right. Geoff's assigned to the Escort of the Key, so he'll be out until ten. And my mother's got a tournament. She warned me that it might go till midnight."

Tomorrow. I'm simultaneously terrified and overwhelmed with excitement. My pussy is slick and swollen.

"I didn't expect it would be so soon..."

"Do you want to do this or not?" His breathing is heavy. He's excited, too.

"Yes, yes, of course."

"I'll pick you up at seven thirty. You'd better be ready for me."

I'm ready now, wet and open and dying to get off. Except that my legs are trembling. I sink down on the sofa. Tomorrow. Somehow, I manage to make it through the next twenty-four hours. I'm dazed with desire, my knickers a sodden mess from the moment I put them on. At work, I nearly give Mrs. Washburn the box with Ms. Simpson's black lace teddy, instead of her WonderHold ExtraFirm girdle. I catch the error (imagine prim Mrs. Washburn opening *that* parcel!) at the last moment. Lucy notices and gives me a dirty look. When she touches me on the sleeve, electricity sizzles through me, straight to my pussy. My whole body is sensitized, pulsing with the current of fantasy on the brink of fulfillment.

Mum has cooked roast beef, normally my favorite, but I can hardly eat a bite. "Are you feeling sick, Maureen?"

"No, Mum, I'm fine. I just had a big lunch. Maybe I'll have a cold plate later." I begin to clear. Mum looks at me suspiciously.

"Are you going out?"

"Oh, yes, didn't I tell you? Cousin Phil and I are going to a movie." I always find that a half-truth is far safer than an outright lie. "I'd better go get ready."

Mum is skeptical. She's not sure she approves of her brother's new stepson, though Phil's always polite and attentive to her. She told me that she thinks he's fast. If she only knew!

"Well, make sure he has you back before eleven, now. Tomorrow's a work day, you know."

"Of course, Mum." By eleven o'clock the Ceremony of the Keys will be finished. By eleven, it will be done, my lifelong desire fulfilled. My heart is beating so hard, I almost expect that she'll hear. "I'll see you later."

In my room I strip and shower, then pull on a soft jersey

that stretches seductively over my breasts and a denim skirt. No underwear; I want to be as close to naked as is possible. My pussy throbs. I'm terribly tempted to touch myself, bring down the level of tension, but I resist. Save it. Save it for Phil and Queen Victoria.

Phil is ten minutes late. I'm ready to kill him when he finally arrives, especially when his grin tells me that his tardiness was deliberate. "Hey, cuz, you look great." He leans over the gear stick to kiss me, and I let him, but when he starts to paw my breast, I pull away. He tastes of Wrigley's chewing gum and whisky.

"Have you been drinking?" I try to sound stern, but his closeness sends my arousal into high gear.

"Just a shot of courage. Or two."

"Well, be careful. The last thing we want is for the police to pick us up."

"Of course, madam."

He drives through the mayhem of London with exaggerated caution, stopping on amber lights, keeping our speed well below 30. It seems to take forever. I glance over at his crotch. He's hard, I'm sure of it, which is a very good sign. I sit back in the bucket seat and try to relax.

It's eight fifteen by the time we arrive at the outer gates of the Tower. Phil flashes his resident's pass at the guard on duty, and we sail through. We park in the common lot, then walk across the Green to the neat row houses that shelter the Yeoman Warders. The Warders and their families are required to live within the Tower grounds. Uncle Geoff's place is dark except for the lamp above the door. Phil looks around nervously before turning his key and letting me in.

"Come on. The wardrobe's on the second floor." He whispers, even though we are clearly alone in the house.

I follow my cousin through the shadowy halls and up the

stairs. I can smell his sweat, his maleness. Juices from my pussy drip down the inside of my thighs.

He knocks at a closed door. I catch my breath; does he expect an answer? In any case, there's no response. The door swings open, and then we are there, in my Uncle Geoff's bedroom, where he sleeps with my new aunt, where he stores the regalia that set him apart from the common mold of man. Phil turns on a dim lamp near the bed.

"There." He points to a plain-looking oak wardrobe in the corner. In a heartbeat I'm standing in front of it, pulling at the handles, but I can't seem to get it open. It's like one of those nightmares where you try to move, to lift your hand and grasp your desire or to flee from your ultimate fear, but you're frozen. All your efforts are futile.

Tears well up. So close. Then Phil grins, reaches into his pocket and holds up a key. "He keeps it locked. Thieves, he says. Each uniform is worth more than a grand, after all."

The key turns smoothly. I fling the double doors open, and there they are: the uniforms. There's the scarlet-and-gold dress uniform, with its snowy white ruff and puffy headdress. A pair of black, patent-leather shoes are aligned carefully underneath.

This gaudy finery doesn't interest me. I'm focused on the un-dress uniform, the sea-blue tunic and trousers with the ruby-red piping spelling out ER—Elizabeth Regina—across the chest. The jaunty hat with its circular brim. It's a chilly October night, and my uncle must be wearing the winter-weight uniform. The sum-mer uniform is wool, too, but light, almost like linen. I reach out a finger and trace the bright trim around the cuff. It feels as though someone is trailing his fingers through the folds of my cunt.

Finally, impatient, I pull my jersey over my head and toss it on the floor, then undo my zip and step out of the skirt. Phil releases an appreciative wolf whistle. I hardly notice. I reach for the tunic, pull it from the hanger, slip my arms into the sleeves, fasten it up to my neck. It's loose, of course. Every time I move, the finely knit fabric brushes over my swollen nipples, fanning the smoldering heat in my cunt into new flame. The cuffs fit snugly. On the shelf I find a pair of spotless white gloves. I pull them on, then consider the trousers.

My cunt is soaked, dripping with desire. In my fantasies, I'm always bent over, my Beefeater's trousers pulled down to bare my bottom to the men waiting behind me. Geoff's pants are way too long, though. Plus, if I bring them anywhere near my raunchy wet pussy, they'll be soaked and stained by my juices and possibly spoiled forever.

That thought by itself almost makes me come. But I cling to a shred of common sense and pass the trousers by. Instead, I reach up to the shelf and pick up the hat. I plant it on top of my tangled, red-brown curls. My hair's so thick that it's a perfect fit.

I turn to face the mirror on the inside of the wardrobe door. I can hardly breathe. The person looking back at me is a stranger, a saucy pixie with hazel eyes and flushed cheeks. Her parted lips look bruised from kissing, fuller and redder than mine. The royal hue of the coat contrasts with the creamy paleness of her thighs. When the placket in the front separates, you can glimpse the fur of her mound. Her hat is perched at an irreverent angle, not straight across the brow the way Uncle Geoff wears it. Under her venerable costume, her body is ripe and open. She lets out a little sigh. She's begging to be fucked.

The tunic reaches to my knees, but I can feel currents of air creeping underneath it, caressing my naked bum. I'm aching to plunge both of my hands deep into my pussy. I imagine those pristine white gloves becoming wet and sticky with my fluids. I think about leaving them, afterward, on the shelf in Geoff's closet to fill up the hallowed space with the common, oceany smell of sex.

Every depraved image makes me hornier. Then I notice Phil's reflection. He's sitting on the bed behind me, staring, his cock jutting from his trousers and pointing straight up at the ceiling. I want that cock like I've never wanted anything.

"Turn around," he whispers. I drag myself away from the mirror and face him. "Open the jacket. I want to see your tits." He grips his swollen organ and it jumps eagerly.

It's hard to undo the covered buttons in my gloves, but I manage. The fabric hangs open, the scarlet calligraphed *E* brushing against one breast, the *R* against the other. Without being told, I cup my tits and fondle them with my gloved fingers. The nappy cotton is soft as velvet. Every touch shoots straight to my clit. I brush my thumbs over my rigid nipples. It's like someone's rammed a thick, flaming candle deep into my cunt. My muscles clench, sending darts of pleasure out to my extremities.

Phil gestures impatiently. "Get over here, wench, and eat my meat."

I'm on my knees in front of him in a trice. I bend over and swallow his whole cock. There are no preliminaries, no teasing. We're beyond that now. Phil moans and grabs my shoulders for support. I work my mouth up and down along his impressive length, savoring the silky texture and salty taste. I can almost feel his hard, slippery rod sliding in and out of my hungry cunt.

As my head bobs, the hat tumbles off into his lap. Now when my mouth reaches his root, I graze my cheek against the hat brim. I have a vision of Phil's come spurting in white curlicues across the navy fabric. My pussy twitches and shudders. I'm ready to explode.

I can't take anymore. I release his flesh with one lingering lick of appreciation and flop onto my chest on the bed, my bum in the air. Phil needs no further invitation. I hear the crackle as he opens a condom package. He parts the back flaps of the tunic and sinks his cock into me in one smooth motion.

He's in deep, so deep. It's delicious, incredible pleasure with a fringe of pain. I squeeze my cunt muscles around his resilient flesh. He moans and pulls out, only to ram himself in again. Groping his way through the wool bunched under me, he finds my nipples and pinches them hard. Now it's my turn to moan.

"Please, oh, yeah, oh…fuck me, Phil, oh, please, yes…"

"You bet I will, you kinky little slut. I've been waiting for this a long, long time."

Oh, and so have I, but now it's worth it. He speeds up his strokes, slamming into me, pulling out, plunging in again, faster and faster, a train puffing and steaming as it hurtles down a hill. No brakes, we're going to crash and we don't care, there's nothing now but his cock in my cunt.

I arch my back, writhing against him, trying to force him deeper still. My clit feels huge and tender; I'm desperate for him to touch it. He releases my tits, but instead of ministering to my poor hungry clit, he grabs my butt cheeks and opens me wider. I'm so close, I'm quivering all over. Just one touch is all I want, all I need.

He does touch me, but not my clit. Instead, he approaches the forbidden tightness of my back door, stroking, circling, then wiggling just the tip of a finger, barely inside. My whole body tenses, on the edge, trembling with terror and lust. He can't, he wouldn't, would he?

Suddenly there's a rush of wind and I'm floating, looking down at my own body, at Phil riding me with all his strength. His jeans are down around his knees. Crumpled blue and scarlet fabric covers my upper back, but I can still make out the ap-pliquéd crown emblem across the shoulders. My bare buttocks swell out from under the tunic, pale and inviting. The dark crev-ice between them is easily visible in this tableau, Phil's meaty cock disappearing into my cunt, Phil's finger poised and pressing against that moist whorl of muscle. I see the Beefeater's hat, discarded, on the floor. My white-gloved hands clutch desperately at the bedspread.

It's the hottest thing that I've ever seen.

There's this moment where time stops. I'm on the peak. Then I swoop back into my body and everything happens at once. Phil pushes his finger into my bum-hole, triggering guilty pleasure too intense to bear. At the same time, he grinds his cock into me, his come exploding in my depths.

It's finally enough. I shimmer, shatter, dissolve into a whirl of sensation. And I don't imagine anything. No dirty pictures. Everything is washed in clean, white light, pulsing in time with the throbbing in my sex.

The striking of a clock somewhere in the house brings me back to awareness. The dead weight of Phil's body is still draped across my back. He's surprisingly heavy. Solid. Without thinking, I count the chimes. At ten, I yelp and scramble up from the bed, dumping Phil on the floor and simultaneously reanimating him.

"Come on! It's ten o'clock. Uncle Geoff will be back any minute."

Phil looks suitably alarmed. I strip off the tunic and hang it back in the wardrobe, trying to smooth out the wrinkles. He retrieves the hat and lays it on the shelf. I tug off the gloves and place them carefully next to the hat. With a twinge of regret, I realize that they do not, in fact, smell of my arousal. Phil grabs the condom and wrapper. I scoop up the pile of my clothes from the floor. We close the wardrobe just as we hear the slam of the door downstairs.

"Come on. My room's across the hall." As we slip into Phil's bedroom, we hear Geoff's tread on the stairs. "Under the covers," my cousin hisses. He lies down and I press my body against his, enjoying the echoes of our recent pleasure. He pulls the sheets over my head. We both hold our breath.

There's a knock on the bedroom door. "Phillip? Are you here?" The door opens and Uncle Geoff is silhouetted against the hall light.

"I'm here. Went to bed a bit early. I've got an exam tomorrow."

"Ah—that's probably a good idea." Geoff takes a step into the room. I tremble, holding onto Phil's hand. What will Geoff do if he discovers our treachery? "Anyway, have you been here all night?" He switches on the light. I cower against my cousin.

Phil sits up, pulling up the blanket so his stepdad won't see that he's fully dressed. "No, I just got home, maybe fifteen minutes ago. Why?"

"Well, somebody left my wardrobe unlocked. The key's in the lock, but it's not turned. Do you have any notions as to who might be responsible?"

I peek out and my heart does a somersault. Uncle Geoff's wearing his Warder's uniform. He sounds so stern, every bit the royal guard. Meanwhile, something pokes against my thigh. I reach down to find that Phil's getting hard again.

"Maybe my mum needed to put something inside and forgot to lock it? Or maybe it was Mrs. Ferguson?"

"Hmm. Well, nothing seems to be gone. But I do like things to be in order. Anyway, I'm sorry to disturb you. Good night, and good luck in your examination tomorrow." He flips off the light, and I let out the breath I've been holding.

"Thanks. Good night." The door closes.

"Wow, that was close." I snuggle against my cousin, stroking his growing erection. "Thanks, Phil. Thanks for everything. That was really fabulous."

He reaches under my arm and clasps my bare breast. His skin

is cool and slightly moist. The bed smells of him, a smell that is now familiar and definitely exciting. I can feel him grinning in the dark.

"Yeah, it was, rather."

"We'll have to do it again sometime." I slip my hand into his pants and give his balls an affectionate squeeze. His cock jumps to attention.

"Well, actually, since you're such a kinky girl…"

"I am not!" Phil insinuates a finger between my buttocks. I can't help gasping.

"As I was saying, since you're so kinky, maybe you'd be interested in trying something else."

"Something else? Like what?"

"Well…" He seems to be shy all of a sudden, but his cock is more swollen than ever. "You work at a lingerie store, right? Corsets, negligees, that sort of thing? Do you ever get to sample the merchandise?"

Light is dawning. "Well, I get an employee discount. And sometimes if something is damaged, Lucy might let me have it." I stroke his silky hardness, imagining the possibilities. "So you want me to dress up in some kind of risqué lingerie?"

"Not exactly." Phil kisses me, a lingering kiss that's full of as much sweetness as heat. "I've never been able to tell anybody else about this, but I know that you'll understand."

All at once I have a clear picture of what he really wants, in full, outrageous detail. My pussy liquefies. I grab his hand and force it between my thighs so he can feel my answer. He gently disengages and slips his cock into me, instead.

The clock downstairs strikes eleven. I realize that Mum's going to give me hell when I finally get home. Right now, though, I'm imagining a longer-term future.

PHONE FATALE

Stan Kent

Sophie Taylor's business card said PHONE FATALE and de-scribed her as a phone-fantasy artiste. Yes, she gave phone sex for a living, but she was so much more than those pur-veyors of grunts and groans, moans and slurps, and cli-chéd "Oh, yeah, baby" platitudes. She had always enjoyed titillating talk and dirty dialogue, often encouraging lovers to describe what they were doing or going to do, and enjoy-ing in return her own erotic musings. Many of her lovers and girlfriends had often joked that she should be a professional phone-sex artiste, but it seemed so remote she'd never taken it seriously. She would still be working as an administrative assistant in an investment bank if it hadn't been for a pair of laddered tights and her boss's secret desire to wear women's underwear beneath his suit.

Sophie checked her bedside clock. It was time. She tossed her magazine to one side, tucked her long legs under her silk-cov-ered bottom, curled up among the pillows, and dialed Jonathon

Stern's private number. She twisted the phone cord around her fingers tightly. His voice was edgy—almost nervous.

"Hello."

"Hello. May I speak to Jonathon?"

The cat-and-mouse game had begun. Sophie knew it was Jonathon. He was her oldest and most regular customer. She'd dialed his private line, to which only he had access, but suggesting that there was an element of doubt was crucial to establishing the upper hand.

"This is Jonathon."

"Hello, Jonathon, it's Sophie. Are you alone?"

She twisted the phone cord a few more turns, imagining the black coils tight around his cock. She was already getting wet. It was her secret weapon. It was why she was so good at phone sex. She enjoyed it more than the client. She was the ultimate phone fatale.

"Yes, yes, I was expecting your call. Let me close my office door and make sure Samantha knows I'm not to be disturbed."

"Yes, Jonathon, you do that. You don't want another woman discovering your dirty little secret."

Sophie relaxed, let go of the phone cord, and sipped her wine until Jonathon returned.

"Sophie...?"

"Yes, Jonathon, I'm still here. I was just daydreaming about you. It's been so long, hasn't it? At least a week. Did you get my last offering?"

"Yes, I did. Thank you so much."

"Are you wearing them?"

"Yes, I am. As you instructed. I have removed my suit and am sitting here in my leather chair in your panties and tights."

"I'm so glad you do as you're told. I wouldn't want to be forced to tell the bank's board of directors that you wear my sexy soiled lingerie under your crisp designer suit as you report on the latest merger and acquisition."

Silence followed, just heavy breathing. It was the game they played. Jonathon liked to wear women's lingerie under his suit, but he relieved the guilt by having Sophie "blackmail" him into his fetish. It was a role she had fallen into and now relished and even perfected.

"Come now, Jonathon, the cat got your tongue? Oh, what a waste. As I remember, you have such a fine, long, and oh-so-nimble tongue. I'd suggest you get it out of that pussy of a mouth and put it were it belongs."

"And where is that?"

His voice was rich and full of expensive tones.

"In your mouth, so that you can talk dirty to me. Isn't that what you want, Jonathon? Aren't there all sorts of filthy things stored inside you that you want to ejaculate into my ear while you wear my cunt-soaked panties and tights?"

"Cunt."

He said the word with such deft precision. He could have been a surgeon.

"That's better, but surely you can do better for the woman who *makes* you wear women's underwear."

"Cunt-licking, cock-sucking slut."

"Flattery will get you everywhere, Jonathon."

"Sexy pussy bitch."

"Oh, my, you have such a way with words. You're getting me wet."

Sophie uncurled her legs and stretched out on the couch. Hearing her prim and proper one-time boss say such things to her was indeed getting her wet and revving up her phone-sex batteries.

"Don't stop, Jonathon. I was just starting to soak my next

pair of undies for you. Keep it up if you want them. You can keep it up, can't you Jonathon?"

"Yes, it's up, it's up, and I'll stick it up you, cunt."

"Promises, promises, promises—you men are all the same."

"I'm not a man."

Sophie fell back on her cat-and-mouse analogy.

"Are you a mouse?"

"No, I'm a man—a man in woman's clothing because you make me wear your slutty lingerie."

"Ah, I see. It's all my fault. Well, indulge me. What are you wearing?"

"Aren't I supposed to ask that, phone slut?"

Jonathon was such a phone-sex veteran. It made Sophie smile.

"Yes, but I asked first. You tell me and I'll tell you. Now go ahead and be honest with me, because I know what I sent you. If you make the slightest mistake, I'll be calling the chairman of the board to expose you as the lying little panty boy that you are."

"I'm wearing your blue satin panties with little white ribbons on the side. Over those I have your lovely black fishnet tights. Nothing else. My toenails are painted red, as you demanded. During a hard day at work it is divine to feel your lingerie under my pinstripe suit and give orders in my silky panties and fishnets with my glossy red toenails, with no one but you knowing. The feeling is too, too debauched. The tension of the tights holding the satin of the panties tight against my cock as I sweat is simply heavenly. It always gives me a constant erection. Now, Sophie, how about you?"

"Me? I don't have a dick. I'm a simple, ordinary girl."

"You're a bad girl. You know what I mean. What are you wearing?"

"I'm wearing silky panties also, only they're black—jet-black satin cut high with ruffles around the legs and waist—almost like camiknickers. You'll look wonderful in them. And then I have on an old camisole top. It's ripped in a few places from where one of my lovers got a bit too aggressive with his teeth, tearing holes in the fine lace. As I turn from side to side the tears catch my nipples, teasing them into tiny little points. I guess those are my erections, Jonathon. My small firm breasts are round, and my nipples get so, so hard, but you know that from the bras and bustiers I've sent you, don't you? I think next time I shall send you this camisole and demand that you wear it under your shirt so that your nipples feel the same torture as mine."

"I look forward to it with pleasure. And speaking of pleasure, are you toying with your clitoris? If I had one and I were talking to me, I would be fingering my little button madly."

Sophie exhaled. Jonathon had the kind of voice, and said the kind of things, that could charm a woman right out of her panties and him right into them, literally.

"Would you like me to?"

"Yes, yes I would. I'd like you to stretch out, spread your legs wide, and slide your hand past those dainty black ruffles, past that dark little bush of yours, part your sticky cunt lips, pull up that softly plump flesh to uncover your prize, and slowly work it between your fingers as you talk to me. Do that, Sophie, do it. Do it for me. Make your panties wet for me so that when I put them on it is as if your cunt were rubbing next to my cock. Do that for me."

"I already was, Jonathon. I'm way ahead of you."

As he spoke, she hypnotically slid her hand under the elastic of her panties, to the folds between her legs. Instead of focusing on her clitoris as he'd demanded, she let her fingers slide lazily into her soft opening, working the tender flesh ceremoniously,

coaxing and teasing the way no man could ever hope to understand. But with Jonathon she came close.

"Does it excite you to think of me wearing women's
clothes?"

"Yes, yes, it does, Jonathon. It excites me to think of you
talking to me, sitting in your office, your staff outside your door,
your suit lying crumpled on the floor, your cock bulging against
the delicate material of my sexy, sodden underwear pressed tight
against your flesh. It's so very erotic, Jonathon, like a forbidden
fruit. I would love to see the outline of your shaft, pulsing and
throbbing underneath the silk, crisscrossed by the bondage of
the fishnets, held captive by them, made to come by them."

The tenor of Jonathon's voice changed. He became almost
serious.

"There are times when I get envious of the women at work.
I watch them walk by, sitting at their desks, crossing their legs. I
know what they're up to. I know they're enjoying the sensuous
power of the nylon held taut against their soft skin. When they
walk, I can hear their thighs brush against each other. I know
what they're doing. I know a woman can pleasure herself just by
crossing her legs when she's wearing panties that slide up against
her pussy, held there tightly by the demanding nylon of those
delicious tights. I know and it makes me envious. Why must
women have all the fun at work?"

"But they don't, Jonathon. Because I make you wear their
cast-off underwear, because I found out your secret. Tell me,
Jonathon. Tell me everything about how you learned you could
wear women's tights and panties to the office."

"Are you playing with yourself?"

"Yes, yes, I am."

"You can, but don't make yourself come, not yet, please."

"Okay, Jonathon, I won't come until you tell me that I can.

I'm just lightly gliding my hand over my pussy. It feels exceptionally good tonight. I'm getting very wet. Would you like to hear?"

"Yes, please."

Sophie held the phone to her pussy and rubbed the handset across her lips, imagining it was Jonathon's lips. She heard him sigh and say what a lovely pussy she had and how he loved her delicious, delicate lingerie. Her body tingled with each lick of Jonathon's electronically processed words. She felt captivated by his fetish, excited by his purposeful precision. She put the receiver back to her face.

"That was very good, Jonathon. I felt your tongue on my pussy, through the silk of the panties, tasting my cunt, tasting my cunt-soaked panties that you will soon be wearing for me. But first, tell me about the first time, when our panty affair began."

"Do you remember that night, Sophie, when I asked you to work late to help me complete a quarterly ending report? It was a Friday and you complained you had a date in the evening, but I persuaded you to help me get through the tedious task with the promise of overtime and a good raise when review time came around."

"Did you want me, Jonathon? Did you want to fuck me?"

"No, heavens no, don't get me wrong, Sophie. I professionally respect you and all the women in my office. I would never use my position to harass you or them. In asking you to work late, I was only trying to get the report done on time. There were no ulterior motives at all. We finished about nine in the evening. The janitors had made their rounds, and everyone had gone home except us. I thanked you for a job well done and bid you good night. I said I'd remain to finish up the last few details. As you turned to leave my office I couldn't help noticing you had a run in the back of your nylons. Being the considerate gentleman that I am, I mentioned the stocking snag. It caused you much consternation since you were heading off on a hot date. You said you had an extra pair of pantyhose—that's what you called them—pantyhose—in your desk. I was intrigued by your comment—excited by the word *pantyhose*—and followed you to your office, watching the ladder in your pantyhose crawl up your calf, up your thigh. You shut the door. I proceeded on to the Xerox machine room to copy the facts and figures we'd worked on, but the only figure I was thinking about was your pantyhose-covered legs and how good that nylon would feel on me. As I Xeroxed away, you came out of your office wearing a different-colored pair of tights. You said goodnight. Once again, I thanked you for your efforts, doing my best not to look at your sexy legs and the blatantly new coverings they'd spawned."

Sophie found herself quickening the pace of her hand across her sex. Increasingly, she found that her fingers lingered longer on her clitoris, toying, more than brushing as she had done in the beginning. She was worried that she should have been saying more, but it seemed that Jonathon was on autopilot. She sighed and let her fingers do the talking.

"So, Sophie, you know what I did, don't you?"

"Yes, Jonathon, I do, but I want you to tell me every detail of what you did next. It sounds sexier coming from you, and it is important that you acknowledge your guilt."

Jonathon whispered, as if in a confessional box. The effect was not lost on Sophie, who found the telling of sexual secrets a potent aphrodisiac.

"I waited until you had left, added a few minutes in case you had forgotten something and returned, and then when I thought it was safe I darted out of the Xerox room and went straight into your office and directly to the garbage can under your desk.

There, in their wrapping, was the old pair of charcoal gray with reinforced cotton gusset."

"And what did you do with my tights, Jonathon?"

Sophie was more orchestra conductor than leading lady. She directed Jonathon down the pathway he wanted to go. This was his confessional and she his conspirator.

"They were so soft, so gossamer-like, and they smelled of your perfume—and—and it was the sense of smell that led me to my discovery. I sniffed at them, following the trail of perfume along the leg until there was a noticeable change in odor—a mixing with a newer, muskier, stronger smell. The odor was the strongest at the crotch where the cotton was still wet with your feminine juices. I realized I had grown erect just standing there with your tights—your pantyhose—in my hand."

"And then what did you do in my office?"

"In no time I was masturbating with your laddered tights wrapped around my cock. I twisted the silky legs around my shaft and held them there with my hand. With my other hand I stuffed the crotch of your tights into my mouth tasting, yes, tasting your juices. I realized then you must have been making yourself wet for your date with all that sexy leg crossing and nylon-covered thighs squeezing together on the firmness of my office chairs. It was obvious to me."

"And what happened, Jonathon? What happened to your nylon-covered cock as you tasted my juices?"

"I came instantly. It was a religious experience—a moment of discovery. After I recovered, I decided to put them on underneath my pinstriped suit. It was then that you returned and found me in the act."

"Yes, it was quite a sight. In my rush to get out of there I'd left my lipstick and makeup, and I wanted to look pretty for my date, so I came back to find you. Seeing you stuffing your impressive cock into my laddered pantyhose was a shock. I didn't know whether to laugh, scream, or cry. I was tempted to make you up like a tarty wench, but it was sufficient to watch you complete the job."

"Yes, you made me put on your tights, and I drove home wearing them. Despite my embarrassment at being caught by you, I was supremely excited. Every little movement sent electric shocks through my body. It was like millions of pairs of tiny fingers squeezing and kneading my legs, my toes, my ass, my balls, my cock. It was a revelation to discover what I had been missing, what women had been enjoying. I quickly regained my erection and I slept in your tights all night long. I still have them, along with many others. I have quite a collection."

"And tonight I shall add to it."

"What pantyhose have you put on?"

"A black pair—sheer to the waist—like the new pair I put on that night that changed both our lives."

"Perfect. Will you please continue playing with yourself?"

"Of course. I'm going to soak my pantyhose just for you."

"They will be the prize of my collection."

"How do you come by them? Besides my supply, do you use your good looks to lure unsuspecting women into leaving their lingerie in your apartment?"

"That is one way. I have refined the laddering of tights into a fine art. I act clumsy, a kiss to the cheek, a slip of the hand, a ring appropriately roughed to catch the delicate material—*blast*—*a ladder*—*damn, I'm so sorry*—and they throw them away. Then it's just a matter of raiding the garbage. I judge how successful my date has been by how wet the crotch of her tights have become. There are many other ways. At the office, I'll often work late and beat the janitors to the women's bathrooms. I find many pairs in the trash, as I'm sure you know. I don't take the chance of being caught wearing them. Another woman may not be as understanding or as accommodating as you."

"And as easily paid off."

"Yes, I do like our arrangement."

"I think of it as a marriage made in heaven. I never really wanted to work in an office. Now I can work at home as a phone-sex artiste. You pay me well to keep quiet about your fetish, and I can afford a steady supply of tights and panties to replace the ones I send to you with my signature scent."

"We do have the perfect relationship. You understand me and I understand you, and together we meet our respective needs. I am like a child on Christmas morning when I rush to pick up the express mail package."

"One day, Jonathon, I might ask you to come and pick up the panties and pantyhose personally so you can have them as freshly soaked as that first pair."

"What a treat that would be, but I am there tonight, Sophie, already in your room, dressed in my silky blue panties and my black nylon fishnet tights. I walk toward you, and you hear the nylon rub together as my legs cross. In the dark, static charges flash across my thighs, electric-blue shocks whipping my legs, matching the sensuous color of the satin of my panties. So urgent is my erection, my cock is bulging through the material, stretching the waistband away from my flat stomach. You are wearing the very same outfit you so seductively described to me. The black satin panties with the ruffles, the black, sheer-to-the-waist tights and the torn-in-all-the-right-places camisole. You are excited to see a man dressed as I am. You squirm on your bed in anticipation. You go to remove your tights, anticipating that we will make love in the most traditional of ways, but I stop you. I push you back down onto the bed. I mount you, opening your nylon-encased thighs as wide as you will let me."

"Yes, Jonathon, I have them wide and around your neck. Do you like the feel of my ankles, covered in black nylon, around your neck? Don't you love that feeling?"

"Yes, yes, I do. The feel of your ankles against my skin makes my cock pulse with the excitement of wanting to come. To squirt my warm release into that smooth satin covering, to feel it ooze between my silky-covered thighs—it is all I live for. Your legs pull me to you, sensing my desire. I settle between them, pressing my fishnet- and satin-covered cock against your mound. I slide my erection over your cunt, up and down, up and down, kissing at your breasts, at your tiny, hard nipples that peek through the camisole. You moan at the decadence of our lovemaking, experiencing wave after wave of rolling orgasm as each little ridge of my dick is amplified by the distinct lines of the crisscross of the fishnet. The material makes my cock feel like the most subtly textured dildo you could ever possess. You moan in ecstasy. You come in tiny, exploding flashes of light with every collision of silky material against material, flesh rubbing on flesh, separated by the smallest of delicious barriers.

"I feel myself building to orgasm and I press harder, more forcefully against you. You strain your cunt around my cock, as if to swallow it. You cannot stop as your pussy shudders..."

Sophie arched on the couch, thrusting her hips skyward, as if she could offer them to Jonathon through the phone system that carried their libidinous words to each other.

"You settle back against the bed, feeling the warmth spread between your legs, soaking my presents even more." Sophie collapsed back to the couch with a sigh and curled her legs up to her bosom.

"Jonathon, you're in the wrong business. You're wasted in banking. I can think of much better deposits you should be making. You make a girl's assets quite liquid."

"Thank you, Sophie. Coming from one so expert as you, I take that as a compliment of the highest order. I can't wait for the next time."

"But, Jonathon, don't you—I mean—aren't you interested in, well, coming?"

"Sophie, although I do so appreciate your concern for my fulfillment, I have an intense erection that I shall nurture all evening. Lying on my bed in my tights and panties, I shall think of you. I shall rub myself against my satin sheets and later, much later, I may orgasm. I may not. I may choose to wait until your gift arrives, and then I shall run from the mail room and come in fountains over your intimate clothing. It is my way. It is the wait, the excruciating wait in my satin and nylons that I treasure so."

"First thing tomorrow, Jonathon. I'll put my panties and tights in the mail."

"And Sophie, if I may, please put them in a sealed plastic bag so that they retain your charming odor."

"No problem, Jonathon. I'll do it right now."

"Goodnight, Sophie. Until the next time."

"Bye, Jonathon."

Sophie lay on her couch, the phone dangling, hand cradled between her legs, pressed tight against her sex by the dual compress of her laddered tights and satin panties. Placing the phone in the cradle, she kept her hand between her legs, relishing the moistness of her cunt. It was a delicious feeling. She now knew she would have to find a lover who wouldn't mind dressing up in some of her lingerie.

But she already had one...

Five more times that night the phone rang, and during each phone fantasy Sophie kept her presents for Jonathon pressed close to her warm body, improving their vintage with every flick of her finger. Each of the calls had their moments, but none kept Sophie on edge as had Jonathon's obsession with female clothing.

At the end of the evening, Sophie was $500 richer and exhausted. The last thing she did before crawling into bed was put her thoroughly damp panties and completely soaked tights into a sealed plastic bag, just as she had promised Jonathon she would.

The next day she didn't mail them, though. They went express delivery all right, personally delivered and worn by Phone Fatale Sophie Taylor for Mr. Jonathon Stern.

I NEED A MAN

Andrea Dale

W hat's it like to fuck a boy?"

Kim and I were lying in a tangle of sweaty limbs and sweaty sheets. I had a bad habit of blurting things out in the postcoital languid daze—usually along the lines of "This isn't working anymore," or, in the case of Kim, "I love you," far earlier than planned.

Kim had gotten used to it since I'd dropped that bomb. But this time, there was more wistfulness in my voice than I'd intended.

"Deciding maybe you're bi, after all?" Her voice was light, but she'd stiffened at my words, her body belying her tone.

"Not that I'm aware of." I tried to match my tone to hers. I felt bad for worrying her. I nuzzled her cheek, smelling sex and cherries. "I'm just curious. Really."

Kim had had a few hetero encounters before she realized she was gay. I, on the other hand, had known I was a lesbian by age five, when I was first caught playing doctor with my best friend.

"Boys are...rougher," she said finally. "Your skin is so soft."
She ran her hand up my thigh, along the curve of my hip.

I shivered. Maybe I wasn't as sated as I thought.

"Maybe it's their body hair," she mused. "And, somehow, they feel stronger. I've been with big girls, powerful girls, but there's something about a man that feels domineering. Not dominating...just more *there*. Oh, and they're less subtle. It's pretty obvious when they're about to come. With a girl, you have to pay attention to the little signals. The way their breathing changes."

She was right—I inhaled sharply when her teeth grazed my collarbone, then let the air out slowly, through my teeth.

"The way the goose bumps rise on their skin when you touch it."

How did she know my skin would do just that as she trailed her fingers across a new slice of untouched skin?

"The way they quiver, just so, when you stroke..."

Now her hand was between my legs, exploring the fresh wetness, and I stopped caring about differences and subtlety and anything that didn't involve my beautiful and talented girlfriend.

I sort of forgot about my question after that. Born in the afterglow, it faded in the reality of daylight and jobs and everyday chores. I suppose a part of me still wondered, but it wasn't keeping me up at night by any stretch.

Kim, on the other hand, has the uncanny ability to squirrel away tidbits of information for later. (She's awesome, for example, when it comes to birthday presents.)

We had a standing Friday night date, sometimes a romantic dinner, sometimes a movie, sometimes a walk on the pier. Tonight, it was eighties flashback night at our favorite club.

I got to Club Addiction a little late, but I didn't see Kim's lavender lace headband with the big bow anywhere in sight. She usually went the Madonna route, all sexy bustier (and who was I to complain?) and fingerless gloves and lots of bracelets. I tended more toward the hair-metal look, with zebra-striped spandex leggings and thigh-high boots.

It didn't really matter. We went there to dance and look at pretty girls.

I ordered a Vodka Sunrise and leaned against the bar to wait for Kim, clinking my fingernail against the glass to the beat of "Don't You Want Me." I smiled hello at a gorgeously androgynous man in a suit à la David Bowie.

No, more like Ultravox, with that slicked-back dark hair and pencil-thin mustache. Warmth pooled in my belly, but from the alcohol. I'd always loved that androgynous look. Annie Lennox at that one awards show had sent me running for my bedroom. But even when it was a male member of a New Romantics group, I'd still felt a frisson of desire—because what if that slender, effeminate guy turned out to be a woman after all, down underneath that natty, light-gray suit?

What if?

I'm embarrassed to say how long it took me to recognize Kim. I politely rejected "his" advances more than once before I heard Kim's husky timbre beneath what I finally noticed was a falsely lowered voice, before I caught Kim's habit of tracing circles against the side of her glass with her forefinger.

Before I saw the oh-so familiar glint of amusement and lust in her blue eyes.

"Want to dance?" she asked again, and this time I agreed.

Usually we went to the club to bop around to the bouncier songs, but Cyndi Lauper's "Time After Time" seemed perfect right now.

Kim had done a great job, I had to say, right down to using a men's aftershave rather that her usual perfume. But when we went cheek-to-cheek on the dance floor, I caught the underlying scent that was so very *her*.

My nipples hardened under my ripped Mötley Crüe T-shirt. I hadn't figured it out, but Kim had put it all together and dug out my ultimate fantasy. I didn't want a boy, not really. I wanted to *pretend* I was with a pretty boy.

The fact that it was someone I loved made it even better.

Then she flexed her hips, and I felt her other surprise pressing against my mound.

"Well, *hel*-lo," I said.

She laughed and nipped my earlobe. "Special present, just for you," she whispered. She slid her hands around my hips and pulled me close, grinding the fake erection against me.

The room spun. Or maybe it was just me, spinning on the heady lust of being in the arms of my girlfriend, who'd dressed like a man to tap into my darkest dreams, a fake cock nudging against my crotch. The promise of sex later or, if we weren't careful, some serious pleasure right here on the dance floor, in front of everyone.

You can't wear panties under spandex. Not even a thong. So the fact was, I knew immediately just how wet I was getting, and given a little more time, when we pulled apart, the rest of the bar would know, too.

"Come home with me?" Kim growled in my ear, still in persona. She punctuated the words with a series of thrusts, and if the question had taken longer, I would've climaxed right there.

"I'll follow you," I said.

Because at that moment, I would've followed her anywhere.

A passionate kiss in the driveway, pressing me up against my car while she groped under my T-shirt. Through the house to the bedroom, her hand on my ass, not pausing to check the mail or top off the cat's water bowl.

There was no question in my mind what I needed to do next.

On my knees, I parted the crotch of her pants and drew out her cock. (Her cock, his cock—it didn't matter anymore. I was lost in the fantasy, stunned by the reality.)

She'd found as realistic a dildo as I could imagine (having not spent any quality time with a hard prick in my life, and pictures aren't the same). The way it jutted out from between her thighs, I could believe she was a man.

Wrapping my lips around the hard rod and smearing my lipstick down it made my nipples so hard, they hurt.

"That's it, baby, suck me." Kim's eyes were half-lidded as she watched me. "You suck it so good."

She stripped off the jacket, but left on the T-shirt beneath. She had smallish, beautifully rounded breasts, but she must have been wearing a sports bra because her chest looked flat, adding to the male look. I moaned around my mouthful.

"You want more, don't you?"

Of course I did. Stupid question. I sat back on my heels and watched her slip off the loafers, kick away the pants. She left the T-shirt on.

We'd never used a harness before, previously content to play with dildos and vibrators and our hands. She wore a pair of men's tightie-whities, concealing the straps beneath. The sight of the fake cock springing from her crotch through the fly thrilled me.

She tugged me to my feet, led me to the bed. I started to lie back, but she shook her head and positioned me on my hands and knees. Of course. This way I could still fantasize, pretend to whatever degree I wanted and needed that she was a he.

I was wet, oh, so wet, but she felt me first with her hand, probing between my lips and then, as I watched over my shoulder, spreading it on the tip of the cock.

Stroking it like a man would.

I shuddered.

Just before she touched me again, Kim tapped the iPod on the night table.

"I need a man," Annie Lennox wailed.

My pussy clenched, a barely there mini-orgasm. Not enough, not nearly enough, but I was astonished nonetheless.

I wanted more. Needed more. If Kim didn't fuck me soon, I might go out of my mind.

She pressed the cock between my lips, rubbing it up and down, hissing as it skidded in my wetness. I imagined that was the best feeling for a man, touching that wet warmth, anticipating being surrounded by it. When she brushed against my clit, I wiggled back, eager for more pressure.

But she slipped away, teasing at my entrance, moving in time with my hips so I couldn't get her to sink in any deeper, either.

Why was she tormenting me so?

Then it hit me.

"Fuck me," I said. The words didn't come easily, but once they left my mouth, there was no stopping them. "Fuck me, please. Fuck me with your big, hard—"

The rest was lost in a gulp of air as she did exactly what I begged for.

I'd had dildos inside of me before, so I didn't expect it to be different or new. I couldn't have been more wrong. This was entirely different. Maybe it was the buildup, maybe it was the vision of Kim in that suit dancing behind my closed eyes. Maybe it was the music, and the memory of those tightie-whities with a stiff cock thrusting out, eager for my mouth.

It was all that and more. It was the way her hands gripped my hips, her fingers digging in almost painfully. It was the soft grunts she made, a sound I'd never heard before.

It was the way she moved, so unlike her normal motion.

Kim's thighs weren't rough like a man's might have been, but her strokes were strong, demanding. Because she used her thighs rather than her hand to drive the cock into me? Didn't know, didn't care.

I reached between my legs, felt the slick rod stretching my lips open, devoured and devouring.

"That's it, baby," she moaned. "Come for me." She'd abandoned all pretense of the lower voice, and the knowledge that she was on the edge, too, was more than enough for me.

I stroked my clit, and as I did, her thrusts changed, short and staccato, and I knew she was coming, too. That's all I knew, because I was thrusting back, burying the dildo in me, and I was coming apart, shattering and reforming around the touch of her hands. The sound of her harsh cries brought me to another orgasm and back to earth, grounded again.

We collapsed together, dildo still lodged inside me.

"I love you," I said, and it wasn't one of those postcoital slips. As she already knew, it was true.

A CUTE IDEA

Rachel Kramer Bussel

It started out as a cute idea, inspired by my boyfriend Neil's close-to-perfect ass. He was naked, his tall, slim body bending over our dresser, burrowing around to try to find the pair of boxers he was sure was buried deep inside, even though he hadn't done his laundry in weeks, maybe months. We'd reached a détente where I left him alone about the state of his dirty clothes hamper as long as he eventually got, or bought, clothes that wouldn't make me crinkle my nose in alarm. He'd done pretty well over the last few months, though he was nowhere near approximating my weekly clothes wash, and he simply laughed when he found my voluminous collection of sexy, lacy, very delicate, expensive panties, garters, stockings, and bras drying in our bathroom.

As I looked at his ass, which is, inarguably, the sexiest part of his rock-hard body (though there was plenty of close competition from his solid chest, strong arms, which he uses to carry me when I'm too tired to walk to the car at night, and, of course, amazing cock), the part I loved to grab, fondle, squeeze, and sometimes spank, an idea came to me. I heard him muttering to himself and knew he was probably out of briefs and even out of boxers, which were a far second in his choice of intimate apparel. "Hey, honey, I have an idea. Why don't you put on a pair of my panties? Maybe those new pink ones, with the bows," I said, remembering our devilishly fun time shopping for the sexy pair, which I'd modeled for him in the dressing room.

He'd snuck in when nobody was looking, then been so turned on he couldn't stop staring at me. I had updated the basic, boring thong I'd been wearing with a pink, lacy, frothy concoction, which featured little bows along the edges that were there purely for decoration. With my shaved, sleek pussy visible through its sheer mesh front (I'd put them on over my little cotton thong), he just had to come a little closer and lick me to orgasm. "I can't resist you in those," Neil had groaned before lunging for me. I giggled quietly but was getting aroused myself. He'd wanted to do it with the panties on, but I'd hissed, "We still have to pay for them!" and so I'd taken them off, he'd feasted on me, pulling aside the thin fabric of the thong to get at my sex, leaving me quaking as I clung to the walls of the booth while a saleswoman pounded on the door. "Miss, you've been in there a long time—we have a line."

"Just a sec," I'd called out, my voice going higher as his tongue plunged deeper. I came, spasming against him, then hurriedly put my clothes back on, walking out with a blush splashed across my cheeks. We'd sheepishly hurried out of the dressing room, and I'd bought that same pair in every color they offered, filling my already overstocked panty drawer to the brim. In fact, my undies took up so much room that some had to go in his drawer, but I knew Neil didn't mind.

He turned to me, though, with a quizzical expression. "What

did you just say?" Even though he'd tried to only twist the top half of his body around, I could see his dick bobbing before him. It was hard, and I gasped in anticipation. This was going to be fun.

"Just that if you're having trouble finding your boxers, which you seem to be, I think you'd look really good in one of my new pairs of panties. You know, the ones that made you so horny you had to go down on me in the dressing room. The ones that let you see my pussy through them. What about me? What if I want to see your cock through your *panties?*" I said, emphasizing the last word and giving it every ounce of humor and taunting it deserved. There's just something about "panties" that makes you long to tease a person who's wearing them, to stare at the outline of them beneath their pants or skirt, to imagine them bunching together between their legs. "Briefs." "Boxers." "Panties." The first two sound solid, secure, upright. The last, silly, a laughingstock, but erotic nonetheless. Now I was determined to see my idea through to fruition.

"Here, I'll show you," I said, fishing out the pink pair and moving so I was standing in front of him. I brushed them gently against his cock, watching it respond to the silky-soft fabric. "You're going to look fabulous and totally fuckable."

"Oh, God, Jen," he groaned as he slid into the panties. Perhaps because I'm tall, like him, topping out at just under six feet, and have a sturdy, athletic body even though I'm pretty slim, those panties fit his body like they were made for him. His hard cock pressed against the sheer fabric in front, outlining it and making it seem even bigger. The little bows, which had been a darling touch on me, looked both incongruous and seductive on his manly frame. The whole thing was ridiculous on one level and ridiculously hot on another. I couldn't really say why, only that once I saw him in my panties, I was hooked. The contrast between the pink, girlish color and his hard, strong cock was striking and all the more alluring because of it. Knowing that the panties turned him on *and* made him squirm just a little made me happy because I was the one who could tip the balance.

"Let's get you in front of a mirror so you can see what I'm so excited about." I dragged him over to our full-length mirror, and there he stood, my tall, curly-haired, thin but muscular boyfriend, 100 percent male save for the panties keeping his dick from sticking straight out ahead. He stared into the mirror as if mesmerized.

"I don't know what to say," he finally managed, his voice a bit breathless. "They feel really good on me, plus they remind me of you." Neil grabbed his crotch, then paused, and instead of grabbing, he let his fingers lightly rest on the image before him. He moved his cock around, from one side to another, as if styling it, then turned to the side to check out his ass, clenching his cheeks tightly together, then relaxing again, as if to make sure the panties truly fit. Maybe he'd figured that underwear made for women would know he had a dick and reject him, rather than the very opposite. They clung to his hips, curved with his cock, yielded to his firm, male ass, as if saying, "Please, pick me. I'm here for you, too." Or maybe that's just me, ever anthropomorphizing.

He turned and reached for me, pulling me close enough so my body brushed against the front of the panties. "But I'm a guy, wearing panties. What does that make me?"

I laughed softly, then reached my hand into the panties to feel his pulsing steel rod for myself. "For one thing, it makes you incredibly sexy and daring. It turns me on to see those on you. Beyond that, it makes you just that—a guy wearing panties. It's not like they have magical powers, right?" I said, thinking I was making a rhetorical statement, but my words lingered in the air, making us both wonder if, in fact, the panties did have a power beyond their usual function. I hadn't thought they'd truly change things beyond framing his ass and outlining his cock, and yet I was suddenly enlivened, like we were playing at something that hinted at subversion, transgression disguised in the form of the frilliest feminine finery.

I knelt down before him and breathed onto the pink mesh encasing his hard-on, then sticking out my tongue to trace his shaft. Certainly, sucking his cock through the thin, barely there fabric of the panties was quite different than getting a mouthful of cotton. The panties weren't really in the way, they simply added to the sensual feel of taking him in my mouth. I felt him swelling within the trapping of the underwear—*my* underwear. The same pair of panties we'd taken home and promptly christened with his mouth right where mine now was. Even though I was the girl down on my knees about to give a blow job, I felt a little bit like a guy as my tongue met the silky fabric.

His cockhead was starting to poke out from the waistband, and I delicately tucked it back in, suddenly only wanting him in my mouth if the panties came too. "Yeah, suck it," he said, but more softly than he usually does. Usually, he calls me all kinds of filthy names that make me moan because I know just how true they are. Neil likes to grab my hair and slap his dick against my cheeks and pretty much fuck my face, which gets me wetter than just about anything. We wait until he's just about to come, then, as if pressing PAUSE, stop, and I get into whatever my position du jour is while he fucks me until I come, and only then is it his turn.

But with the panties on him, somehow, tacitly, our roles had changed. I was the one fucking *him* with *my* mouth while he waited to see what would happen next. Maybe the role reversal had come about because I'd been the one to suggest this venture

into panty play, though my suggestion had initially been innocent enough. What girl doesn't want to see her guy's ass framed
in the most fetching way possible? But once I had, my cute little
idea had taken on a life of its own, a life that now had the blood
pumping through my body as I pictured Neil in panties beneath
jeans, beneath suits, beneath shorts. Neil in panties at his family's house for Thanksgiving dinner, Neil in panties at some work
cocktail party, Neil in panties on the subway. Neil in my panties,
doing my bidding, trying to ignore the ache down below as the
silky fabric teased him with its slippery siren song.

In a way, sharing my panties was an equal-opportunity adventure. I was showing him who really kept Frederick's of Hollywood and Victoria's Secret in business. Sure, everyone thinks
it's about guys jerking off to the come-hither poses of the sun-
drenched models, but those of us who take our lingerie seriously
know the truth. It's all about the way it feels when it caresses our
skin—and why should guys miss out?

But the real truth was that no matter what Neil was thinking,
I was thinking that he'd never looked better than in my panties, and made sure I showed him my appreciation with every
lick, suck, and swallow. Eventually, I eased the soaked panties
down enough to take his cock fully into my mouth, keeping the
mesh bunched around his balls. He was remarkably still, letting
me run the show, and when I looked up at him while I had his
entire length buried down my throat, his eyes were glued on me.
I smiled as best I could, then returned to what I was doing. It
almost felt like a threesome between me, him, and the panties.

"Jen, you're gonna make me come if you keep doing that. Is
that what you want?"

Talk about a trick question, if there ever was one. Of course
I wanted him to come. In my mouth. But also in my pussy. And
also on the panties. Everywhere at once, but that would be

demanding the impossible. So I made a sacrifice to the altar of my newfound friend, my panties, which I'd already started to think of as his pair—after all, how could I wear these particular beauties again knowing I wasn't fully doing justice to them? I gave his dick one final lick, then eased the panties back over him. They were totally wet and clung to his hard pole. I stroked him, wrapping my hand around his panty-covered cock and applying pressure with my thumb right at the head. He no longer seemed concerned about any possible impropriety about wearing something that belonged to me; no, from the look on Neil's face, all he cared about was his impending orgasm. I worked the panty/penis combination for just a few more strokes, until he came, his seed bursting into my hand through the thin material.

When we'd both recovered enough to talk, we moved over to the bed. Neil rolled over onto his stomach and I again admired his ass, this time with the pink not so taut but pressed against his cheeks as if he'd been wearing them under his clothes all day. I lay my hand over him and squeezed gently, and he shuddered beneath me. "I guess you'd better look for those boxers," I said, not sure whether I was joking or not.

He turned and looked at me for a long time, then licked his lips, something he only does when he's admitting that I've been right. I can count the number of times it's happened since we started dating, which is why I make a special note of it. "Well, Jen, I was thinking that maybe since these are, well, out of commission for the moment, I could borrow another pair of yours. Just till I find my boxers."

The corners of his mouth curved up into the grin I can never resist. "Just till you find your boxers, of course," I said knowingly. "As long as I get to pick the pair," I said, already envisioning my white lace frilly bikinis with the pink daisies on them, the ones that always made me feel like an innocent schoolgirl at first, and then a very naughty schoolgirl when I realized that I was getting off on the feeling.

"Of course," he said, trying to cover his laugh. He rolled onto his back and I saw he was starting to get hard again. In my mind, I was already buying him his own panty wardrobe, picturing us donning matching pairs and heading out on the town. But I didn't want to get too carried away. One step at a time and all that. I can tell you one thing, though: Now that I've seen him in my undies, I'll never look at Neil's ass the same way again.

HIGHER AND HIGHER

T. Hitman

Roni was hot.

Black low-cut top; black skirt, with sparkly piping along the slit that glittered when she moved, reflecting the soft glow from the strings of Christmas lights draped around the headboard's slats. Black nylons, high heels, also black, with just the right amount of fuck-me quality without looking cheap. Her mane of blond hair and those plump, delicious, apple-red lips completed the illusion. Pure class.

Roni was a real lady, even though what she was doing to him wasn't particularly ladylike. And then there was that whole penis hiding inside her skirt thing to consider.

"Do you want me to go higher?" she cooed. Her voice, too, challenged Nate's illusions.

Higher than what? Nate briefly wondered, lost in the moment. What felt like hours ago, Roni had unlaced his work shoes and removed them. Instead of wrinkling her nose and bitching about the sweaty haze emanating off his black-socked size twelves like Brigitte would have, Roni had pressed her pretty nostrils into the damp cotton of his toes, inhaling their buttery stink with relish. Nate—he'd lied to her, saying his name was Nathaniel—had watched, mystified, as she turned the guilt all masculine, athletic, and mostly heterosexual American males are forced to endure when asked to remove their shoes before entering another person's house into a unique kind of sexual foreplay. That embarrassment when caught off guard is worse than when a guy discreetly tries to sneak out a fart, only to unleash a cannonade of thunder into mixed company when the conversation suddenly and at the worst time possible skips a beat...*bam!* Worse than forgetting to slap on deodorant on a miserably humid day, the same day when the air conditioning at work coincidentally decides to shit the bed.

To Nate's surprise, Roni had loved his feet.

He'd felt the mildly painful scrape of her nails in the thatch of chestnut hair along his ankles as she'd liberated him of his sweaty socks. Warm air had gusted across the sensitive flesh of his naked toes, and then she'd slid her tongue into the cheese-filled canyons between them.

The sensation of having his feet rubbed and licked, especially in their present state after eight hours of drudging work, sweaty and trapped in his shoes, had teased the erection in his pants one step closer to unloading on its own. He'd been hard almost from the moment she'd opened the door and welcomed him into her apartment. Hell, "Nate" had boned over their meeting on the computer, when he'd seen that Roni was passable for a female. A woman who really wasn't one at all. Nate wasn't really a Nate but a Peter, so somewhere in all that fiction, the scales balanced out.

"Do you want me to go higher, stud?" she repeated, pulling Nate out of the spell of thoughts he'd fallen prey to.

Without permission, her sexy talons inched past his ankles, into the cuffs of his khaki slacks. There, they probed his hairy calves. No woman had ever worshipped Nate's legs before this. Four years of college sports—baseball, ice hockey, and jogging—had transformed his legs into those of some minor Greek deity. A dozen more years playing the same sports recreationally had kept them magnificent.

"Sure," Nate stammered.

Roni tugged on both leg cuffs. "You're sure?"

Nate nodded.

"Then take off your pants."

She reached for his belt, his zipper. Nate jolted on the bed and fumbled to accommodate before she got there first. Roni's manicured hand pulled back, as if shocked away from passing too close to an open flame.

Nate took a heavy swallow, only to find his mouth had gone uncomfortably dry. He unbuckled his belt. Unzipped his pants. Pushed them under the hard square of his muscled ass. Roni took over from there, peeling them down his legs and off his feet.

Nate settled back on the pillow and loosened his tie. He undid the buttons of his dress shirt and spread the two halves, hoping the action would help him breathe easier. He narrowed his eyes. Through the slits and in the wan glow of the Christmas lights, she could have been a hot piece of choice, legitimately female tail licking around his ankles and across his hairy shins.

"You have killer legs," Roni said.

Her voice, Nate told himself, was just like Kathleen Turner's: deep and smoky hot, intoxicating like whiskey. Not that of a male. Males didn't have tits like Roni's.

Roni stroked and licked his legs up to the knees, showing them the same attention she'd given to his feet.

"Higher?"

Nate moaned a breathy "Fuck," and stretched. His cock, rock hard and begging to be touched, jammed its teary Cyclops eye against the elastic waistband of his black boxer-briefs. Nate reached down and adjusted it. Up until the point when he'd lost his pants, he'd kept his left hand in the pocket. This had accomplished two objectives: It had allowed him to play a discreet game of pocket pool with his package, and it had kept the gold band on his ring finger hidden.

Higher? Just how much higher? Nate wondered. His knees? No, judging by the sparkle in Roni's hypnotic blue eyes, she'd meant his crotch. Those eyes were too blue to be anything other than contacts, reminding him of the many lies they'd both willingly spun en route to making the encounter happen. But his crotch...there could be no lying about its intentions. Dick stonehard, its head poking out from under cover of a noose of elastic. Dripping precome like a leaky faucet. Balls, so big and meaty and loose—so full, they felt almost painful.

Who was Nate lying to more when he hesitated, Roni or himself? Did he think when he'd IM'ed her in the chat room that her rubbing on his big, sweaty feet would be enough for either of them, or as far as they'd go once they connected?

Nate coughed to clear his throat and nearly gagged on a sour, nervous taste, the taste of empty stomach and peppermint. He'd popped a breath strip onto his tongue during the drive to Roni's apartment. That strip was the only thing in his gut since a second cup of coffee and half a sandwich at lunch, during an afternoon that now felt ages in his past.

"Fuck," Nate groaned again.

Not an hour earlier, he'd been like millions of other sorry, everyday bastards in America. In his mid-thirties. White. Marginalized. The hangman's noose of a tie choking tighter around his neck with each passing day. Trapped in a nowhere job—assistant office manager of a small insurance company. A drone. A peon. With a wife who'd lost all interest in him sexually and, even more crushing, personally. A wife who bitched about every minor detail of his presence in the house they could barely afford to pay the mortgage on. The hairs he left in the bathroom sink. How he sometimes forgot to lower the toilet seat. His stinky feet.

"I think you're really handsome," Roni interjected, cutting through the chaos of the thoughts, emotions, and panic tumbling through his insides. She scooted higher between his spread legs, almost to the region of his groin now causing so much confusion for him. But not to grope his cock and his hairy, itchy nuts, which felt swollen to the size of inner tubes by a rush of primal juices desperate for release.

No, Roni cupped his cheek. Those apple-red lips curled into a seductive smile, and this close, even though Nate could see the Ron who hid behind Roni's façade...

He/she was still intensely beautiful.

"If you're not ready, we could—"

"Higher," Nate ordered, seizing Roni's hand. He kissed its palm, smelling the sweetness of her soap and the sweaty dregs of his own foot odor. He'd marked her with his musk. She was his now, and the concept of not going forward, carrying out the acts he'd really come here for even if he couldn't freely admit it in words, terrified him worse than any fear of actually making it happen.

Nate re-aimed her hand and placed it between his legs. The room erupted in a Fourth of July fireworks display that only he could see. He moaned. Her fingers walked. Nate's entire body tingled with pins and needles, as if his heart were no longer at the center of his being because his cock had taken its place.

Roni went higher. By going lower.

It wasn't the first time Nate had gotten his dick sucked, just the first in a very long time. The first delivered by the lips of a woman who wasn't a woman, exactly. She *was* a woman, he silently lectured that inner voice. She was beautiful. Better than her hotness, she appreciated a man's body, even a beaten, broken schlep like him.

Nate settled back with his arms behind his head and a lusty grin on his face. Roni...she freed his dick and made love to it with her mouth.

Earlier that day in the men's room, after Nate Who Was Really Pete had finished draining his lizard into the urinal's perfumed blue cake, he was struck by his own reflection. Struck by how handsome he was, something he hadn't tom-turkeyed over since college, when he was the kind of dude who got to fuck the ladies two, sometimes three at a time. A jock. A stud.

Nate—the name he'd given Roni over the computer—*was* handsome, he'd conceded to his reflection, wiping his hands, staring into the mirror. He still kept his hair in a neat athletic cut. Even that swarthy, perpetual five o'clock shadow on his neck and cheeks was sort of sexy. Some chicks loved that on a dude. Some dudes, too. Nate had let a dude go down on him once, in an adult bookstore. A few years earlier. It had been the best head of his life, but he'd suffered for it. *A dude.* He'd let another dude lick his hairy nuts, gobble his wad, straight from the spout. Burn-in-hell time, folks, if you believed the religious crazies (and because of his upbringing, a small but vocal part of Nate—less than 1 percent, all told—did).

But Nate Who Was Really Pete had never forgotten the ease of connecting with a willing male mouth. You walk in. Whip it out. Squirt your yogurt down some stranger's throat. Zip up and strut away, big balls swinging proudly, albeit lighter. But the idea of doing that again to a dude came with too much personal baggage for him. Only problem was that other dudes were the only source for a dude like Nate to find such acceptance, such instant brotherhood. Just like a game of pickup hoops or hardball, only with oral sex as the sport being played.

He couldn't do a dude again, but he could do…

…*a dudette.*

Roni eased Nate's boxer-briefs down and over the aching lump between his legs. Nate's cock catapulted against his stomach with a hard, electric slap. Warm air gusted over his balls; as he moved to accommodate her stripping him of his underwear, their sweaty smell assaulted his nostrils. Raw. Powerful. Primal. The ripe stink of a real man's balls.

Roni didn't balk over the musty stink of his sac any more than she had his feet. She took him by the shaft, gently teasing its pitted column with her nails. She kissed the head. Licked the gummed-up piss hole. Tickled the shaft with her tongue. Nate's mouth dropped. His eyelids sagged under the weight of a complete and total mind-fuck of joyous sensations. He just about busted when his left nut vanished between Roni's lips.

Eyes half-closed, Nate grunted a blue streak of expletives. This was better than his college fuck-fests, watching one girl savage another with long, wet laps while yet a drunken third hummed on his bone. Better than the quick suck-and-squirt in the video booth. Better than all of it and everything he'd ever experienced.

Roni licked his sweaty balls from front to back. She even brushed his asshole, another first for Nate.

As promised, Roni moved higher, taking his length between her lips. Nate's cock vanished into her throat, all the way to the lush mat of his pubes. And she kept on sucking, taking him right to the edge of the abyss.

But instead of falling, as his weighty balls unloaded, Nate rose higher. He pushed his cock all the way in, deep enough to make her gag. His hairy ass muscles clenched, his nuts pulled up, and the sensation, he would later recall, was like levitating. Floating up from the bed.

Roni, he was happy to discover, hadn't planned to waste his seed. No spitting it out into the bathroom sink like Brigitte did on those rare occasions (like his birthday) when she forced herself to honor him with a blow job. No, Roni swallowed him down, licked Nate clean, and, when she was finished, dabbed the tip of a manicured pointer at both corners of her apple-red lips, not a single drop wasted.

Nate's first instinct normally would have been to boogie. To bolt. The old *screw, then flew,* as he and some of his pals at work were known to chuckle when their conversations entered locker room territory.

Briefly, he wanted to. Tuck his cock back into his underwear, pull on his stale dress socks, maybe even toss a bill onto the bureau as he beat feet out of the apartment, making no eye contact with the *her* that was really a *him.* But the Nate Who Was Really a Peter gazed into those hypnotic faux blues, then stared down at the swollen monster between his legs. It hadn't gone down after spitting up its batter. His dick wanted, needed, more.

So did Nate.

Roni smiled and licked the sensitive trigger of nerves lining the underside of Nate's cock. "You can fuck me if you want."

Nate hadn't considered such a thing.

"I have a sweet, tight pussy..."

Roni released his length and returned to that balancing act

atop her high heels. She half revolved, putting her curvy ass directly in front of his line of sight. Slowly, seductively, she lifted her skirt, higher and higher. The revulsion Nate worried would punch him in the guts at the revelation afforded by this tea-bagged view never came.

Pussy, asshole, man-cunt, whatever it was...it was beautiful, just like its owner. Hairless and pink. A sweet, pretty pink pussy, and he planned to fuck it.

Roni tossed a condom Nate's way. He tore the foil packet open and rolled the lubricated skin over his dick.

Nate had eaten a chick's asshole before, and though he hesitated at first, after that first tentative lick, he began to feast on Roni's pucker like a starving man presented with the best meal of his life. The mind doesn't ever forget what time tries to dull; though he hadn't licked an asshole since his college days, Nate recalled the bitter, addictive taste well enough to realize there wasn't any difference. Man, woman, Roni...they all tasted great.

Nate penetrated her from behind, riding her doggie-style to his second climax of the night and Roni's first. As he collapsed on top of her, Nate pulled himself higher, until their faces were even.

And then he kissed her.

BIRTHDAY GIRL

Jason Rubis

Ray had found the evening so far a bit of a trial, but when Susanna finally emerged from the bedroom, she looked so excited and happy that he felt like a prick. It wouldn't kill him to be a little supportive.

"Done already? So let's see him."

"Her," Susanna said primly, stepping to one side of the door. "Don't call him 'him.' Sweetie, come on out."

The curtains parted and a girl emerged, shoulders up, hands knotted nervously under her belly.

Ray nodded. "Nice."

"Nice?" Susanna said, laughing shortly. "Just nice?"

Ray was annoyed. What do you want me to do, he thought, hump him right here in the living room? But Donny was a nice kid, this whole thing apparently meant a lot to him. So Ray said, earnestly, "Really nice. Seriously, man. I mean, if I didn't know, I swear…"

Donny colored through his makeup. "Thanks," he whispered, looking at his feet.

He did, in fact, look nice. He might not have been 100 percent passable, but Ray had seen plenty of real girls who didn't
look as good as Donny did now. Susanna had him in one of
her black cocktail dresses; he was just close enough to her in
build—surprisingly small and slender for a guy—that he could
wear it, though it was a bit tight in places. Most of the prep time
had been spent on his heavy black hair, teasing it out so it hung
in a loose haze about his shoulders. Susanna had made him up
to accent his high cheekbones and his narrow, dark eyes. She
had limited his jewelry to a modest bracelet and a pearl choker.
His fingernails had been painted maroon.

Ray, in the midst of proposing a drink to celebrate, noticed
something.

"Where's his shoes?"

"Oh, we've got 'em in the bedroom," Susanna said, bustling
around the kitchen looking for the corkscrew. "You have to do
his toes before we go."

Ray forced a laugh. "What?"

"He doesn't have to," Donny murmured.

"Yes, he does, Donny. It's all right. He does mine all the time.
He's good at it. He likes doing it. Ray, go on, get the polish from
the bedroom. Hurry up, it has to have time to dry. You can have
a glass of wine later."

Ray seethed. The idea of painting Donny's toenails was not,
in itself, hideously distasteful to him, though it was nothing he
would have chosen to do. Neither did he particularly mind that
Donny now knew he sometimes painted Susanna's toes; even so,
this wasn't the first time Suzi had blithely thrown out personal
information. How would she feel if he started babbling to her
friends some night about the handcuffs she liked—very occasionally—to use?

But his choices were limited: Either he stormed out of the

apartment like a little kid or he let it pass. He could, technically, demand to see Susanna in the other room and have it out with her, but poor Donny already looked as though he wanted to disappear into the floor.

"It's okay," Ray told him, giving his shoulder a squeeze that at the last minute he turned into a playful shake. "Sit down, Gorgeous. We'll get you fixed up in no time."

Susanna gave Donny a glass of wine, then disappeared into the bedroom with a glass of her own and her cell phone, to "rally the troops." While she chattered and giggled, Ray gathered the necessary items for his own task. He tried not to look at Susanna as he snatched up the bottle of polish and rejoined Donny.

Donny seated himself on the couch, and Ray sat cross-legged on the floor in front of him. Donny had nice enough feet—just a little bigger, Ray thought, than they'd probably be if he were a girl. The sole of one rested on a folded towel on Ray's lap.

"You really don't mind? I'm really sorry. See, we bought sandals for me today. If I knew Susanna was going to do this, I would have just bought pumps." He gnawed a fingernail. "My feet don't stink, do they?"

Ray smiled good-naturedly. "They smell like flowers." They did, actually. All of Donny smelled like flowers. Like he had been pickled in them.

Donny flinched as Ray applied the brush. "Don't tickle! Please?"

"It won't tickle. It only touches your nail, see?"

"I know, but when I see women get their toes done, like in the nail salons? I always think it'd tickle. My sister used to tell me she'd get her girlfriends to do my toes and it'd tickle. Like torture. Like threatening me with torture. Is that stupid? Oh, God, I can't look."

"It's okay."

Far above Ray's head came the sound of wine being breathily sipped. "You're really nice," Donny said softly. "You're being, like, really nice to me tonight. Thank you."

"It's okay," Ray said again, a little absently. Now that he was actually doing it, he enjoyed the process of painting Donny's nails, just as he enjoyed doing Susanna's. It was strangely absorbing work, slowly filling in each little blank space with its coat of maroon. The polish had a slight chemical smell that mixed with the flowery scent that came from the rest of Donny. It didn't make Ray dizzy, but he inhaled as though hoping it would.

"Where are you guys going tonight, anyway?" he asked.

"The Ambrosia...don't you know? You're coming, too?"

Ray shook his head. "Don't think so." He hadn't planned to go in the first place; he had gone to plenty of gay clubs with Susanna, and they were always an okay time. But tonight was going to be a whole different crowd than he was used to, and he was still irritated. "I'm a little tired tonight, so I'm just gonna..."

"What? No!" Donny almost dropped his glass. "You have to come! Ray! It's my birthday, and I'll feel so bad—I'll think it's 'cause Suzi made you do my gross feet and I saw you almost had a fight and now like you're mad at me, *Ray!*"

"Okay, okay, all right." Ray patted Donny's foot. It registered in a dim part of his mind that he had almost said, "All right, honey."

"You'll come?"

"Sure, I'll come. What the hell, right?"

"You *promise?*"

"Cross my heart," Ray laughed, crossing it. "Pinky swear, okay? Now calm the hell down, okay? Suzi'll think I'm murdering your ass out here."

As he bent his head to get back to work, Donny's hand slid down and caressed his cheek, the fingers creeping down to feel his jaw, then upward to play briefly with his hair.

Ray, unaccountably, felt his face heating up. He glanced up and saw Donny smiling down at him, fingering a strand of his own hair as though trying to rub off on it some essence he had picked up from Ray's. Ray was the one who looked away, but that meant nothing.

"You get a kiss tonight," Donny promised. "'Cause it's my birthday. 'Cause you're a nice guy."

"All right. That's cool." Ray was aware that he was being flirted with. That didn't mean anything, either, he told himself.

Donny's toes squeezed together and pushed a little, applying pressure through the towel onto Ray's leg.

They arrived at the Ambrosia at 11:30, with two of Suzi and Donny's louder friends in tow. By the time they had all paid cover and ordered the first round of drinks, Ray had decided the wisest course of action would be to install himself in a corner and get quietly drunk on domestic beer. This was a tactic that had served him well throughout much of his adult life when faced with difficult social situations. It was easy enough to put into action; as birthday girl and drag virgin, Donny was the center of attention. Nobody bothered at all with Susanna's mean old het boyfriend.

Most if not all of the people surrounding Donny at the corner they had staked out were crossdressers or some variation on the theme. They ranged from shrieking fiftysomething queens to doll-like beauties who seemed to glide rather than walk on their six-inch heels. Every one of these women, Ray mused, every one of them is a man underneath. He found the words had a peculiar unreality; no matter how many times he said them in his head, he couldn't seem to connect them with the people in front of him.

When Susanna first started taking him to places like this, five years before, he had spent a great deal of time wondering whether he could in fact go to bed with one of these people. Since then he had come to terms with the answer, which he found to be a resounding *yes*. It hadn't really mattered, since the opportunity had never come up.

Donny was flushed and happy, something that Ray found pleased him. As the drinking went on, and as Donny and several hangers-on disappeared several times into the restrooms (twice to the men's room, once, to general hilarity, to the women's), returning a little more unsteadily each time, he became louder, more aggressive than Ray had ever seen him. He made extravagant gestures, fluttered his lashes, blew kisses at strangers. It was as though he was now getting used to the new persona he was wearing. It allowed him to do things.

Several times he called attention to his feet, referring to Ray as his "pedicurist." Ray, himself now pleasantly toasted, smiled and lifted his bottle to gradually diminishing cheers.

Finally, he had to make a trip to the bathroom himself. When he emerged, Donny was waiting for him. By now, the featured DJ had taken the stage at the rear of the club, and the place was full of pounding, crashing music.

Ray smiled and nodded and made to walk past Donny back to the bar. Donny wasn't having it. He shook his head and grabbed Ray's wrists, pulling him with surprising force toward the dance floor.

Ray shook his head no. As in, Oh fuck no. No way, no, no, no. Donny, grinning wildly, nodded and lunged forward to gnash his teeth in Ray's ear. "Dance me f'm'birthday," he said, or something similar.

Well, why not? Give the other partyers a good laugh, give Suzi something to tease him about for the next year. Besides, if he said no, he had a pretty good idea of the tantrum that would result.

When they reached the edge of the dance floor, Donny bent to undo his sandals, nearly falling over in the process, and handed them to Ray. Then, barefoot, he began dancing. His movements were, unsurprisingly, not very coordinated, but soon he settled into a simple, undemanding rhythm that he worked furiously, whipping his hair around and peppering the air with spastic-fingered hand jive. Ray was reminded of go-go dancers in sixties movies. He laughed and applauded, Donny's shoes bouncing on their straps as he brought his hands together. The other dancers looked vaguely annoyed—these people didn't know Donny; they wanted to display their moves and work off their highs. The Asian boy in the dress and the big laughing white guy were cramping their style.

That, perversely enough, persuaded Ray to start dancing himself. He had never been a good dancer, never really enjoyed it, but the beer he'd consumed helped a great deal. He used Donny's shoes, one in either hand, as a professional dancer might use batons or flags. This had the pleasing effect of clearing a larger space around them.

Donny laughed and put his arms around his neck, pulling him downward. Ray, still dancing, grinned down at him. "Kiss," Donny said, just loudly enough to be audible. The smell of liquor wafted up into Ray's face. "Birthday...kiss."

Kiss. All right. Sure. If he was going to dance with him, there was no logical reason why he shouldn't let the guy kiss him. But an honest part of him knew this wasn't going to be any little peck on the cheek, and it wasn't. Donny pressed his mouth to his and, after a moment of greedy sucking, thrust his tongue in. At the same time, he reached down and groped Ray's crotch, squeezing adeptly at the erection he had apparently known he would find.

Ray made a gargling sound. Suddenly, Donny's weight was off his shoulders and he was dancing again, giggling and sticking his tongue out suggestively. Now his dancing suggested not a go-go girl but a stripper high on aphrodisiacs. He gyrated his hips and dragged his fingers through his hair and licked them ecstatically. When he began bumping his hips rhythmically at Ray, staring at him with hooded eyes and mouthing four-letter words, Ray knew it was time to go.

He managed to slip into the crowd of dancers before Donny could get a hand on him. He intended to go back to the bar first and say something to Susanna, but it was hopeless—by now, the main Saturday night crowd had assembled. It was all he could do to get out the main door. Suzi would just assume he had gotten sulky and gone home, as usual. It wasn't like she couldn't get home without him.

As he lifted a hand to hail a passing cab, he realized he was still holding Donny's shoes. "Oh, shit," he groaned.

He opened the door of the cab, hesitated. Donny would be okay. He probably would have spent the rest of the night barefoot, anyway. Hell, he was high as a kite on something. He wouldn't even notice his shoes were gone.

Then a gleam of broken glass caught Ray's eye. Broken bottle—no, bottles. A lot of them. Suddenly, the street seemed lined with the fucking things. It was like someone had come out with a sack of broken glass and strewn it all over the place.

"Hey, man," the cabby snapped. "Hey, you getting in or what?"

Donny crying with bleeding feet. Ambulances. Hospitals. Tetanus shots were supposed to hurt like hell.

Ah, fuck.

As the cab pulled away a figure stumbled out of the club's door. Donny.

"Watch out," Ray cried, at unnecessary volume, waving the shoes with both hands. "Glass! Broken glass!"

Donny waited obediently until Ray reached him. "Where are you going?" he asked. He was weaving a little, but he seemed nowhere near as high as he had been a few moments before.

"Home. Look, I'm sorry. It's okay, you didn't…" His own head had cleared considerably, but this somehow didn't make thinking any easier.

"Look, I'll talk to you. Next time you come over. Happy birthday, okay?"

"I want you to come home with me."

This didn't entirely surprise Ray. He said, "What?" anyway.

"Come home with me," Donny said and touched his shoulder. "I want it for my birthday. I know," he went on after Ray stared at him, "I'm just a fucking brat, right? Dance with me, kiss me, paint my toes, fuck me. But, hey, you only get one birthday a year, right?

"And you want to, too…don't you?"

Ray inhaled deeply. "Yeah," he said finally. "I do."

Susanna wouldn't mind. Miss You Pay Half the Rent but We're in an Open Relationship. Hell, it would turn her on. If he told her about it. But he wouldn't.

"One night," Donny said, and standing on his toes, planted a kiss on Ray's chest.

He put his shoes on at Ray's insistence, and they hailed another cab. Ray wondered what he was getting himself into. What was this going to be like?

But he already knew, he told himself. For as long as it lasted, it was going to be wonderful. It was going to be delicious, like the first cold beer of the evening.

And afterward… Well, he had never been one to stop at just one beer, not since the first time he'd tried one, back before college. Settling into the cab next to Donny, he found himself remembering that first beer—the way he'd brought the foaming glass to his lips, the smell, the strange longing the smell woke in him, a hunger mixed with thirst. He remembered how he couldn't wait to get it in his mouth and swallow. He'd never be that young again.

THE PRINCESS ON THE ROCK

Elspeth Potter

Mariamoni's head lolled as the soldiers carried her bejeweled litter past the silent villagers, toward the sea. The distant ritual chanting seemed muffled, as if her head had been wrapped in wool.

The soldiers staggered in the deep sand, and the tiara she wore slipped over one eye. She could smell smoke and incense and the soldiers' sweat. They halted and a shrill ululation tore the air. Through the haze of soothing magic, Mariamoni began to feel stirrings of distress. They were singing her elegy. With the last vestiges of self-control left to her, she submerged herself in the magic again. She was going to die. What point was there to suffering any more than she already had?

The bonfires on the shore roared. The soldiers carried her litter past each one of the three while the priests chanted. She coughed from the smoke, wincing away from the scorching heat on her face. Each of the three attendant priests marked her with oil above her manacled wrists and on her feet and forehead. The oil smelled like fish. She smelled like fish now. Like food. Food for the Monster.

If Mariamoni could speak, she would denounce her uncle and denounce his syncophant priests who had brought her to this; but she could not speak, and by the time the magic wore off, all of the spectators would be gone. The soldiers climbed the ancient carved steps and slid her from the litter onto the rock's summit like a filet from a pan. Someone plunged a flaming torch into a waiting bracket somewhere above her head. A soldier took hold of her arm and stretched it out. Half-blinded by the torch, she couldn't see what he was doing. When metal clashed, she screamed.

The chanting ceased; the magic haze whipped from her mind. Her right wrist was manacled to the rock. Mariamoni closed her eyes. She did not scream as her left arm was pulled out straight and chained down; she would not give her uncle the satisfaction. Her ankles were last; the soldier removed her silken slippers first, then her anklet of tourmalines, given her by some suitor she no longer remembered.

The soldiers descended from the rock with a rattle of armor. The High Priest spoke to her; she ignored him, staring instead up at the stars, not allowing herself to cry, rigidly controlling her roiling stomach. She felt the sharp vibration as the priest tapped each of her bonds with a small hammer; then he departed, his sandals scuffing on the stone steps. An eerie silence descended; she could hear only the roar of greedy flames for a time, then, in the distance, feet scuffling on the path that led back up to the fortress that had once been her father's and now belonged utterly to her traitorous uncle.

The Monster would come just before dawn. The night stretched endlessly before her. Desperately, she endeavored to distract herself with thoughts as far from the rock as possible.

At Midsummer, Mariamoni had worn a gown of silver tissue with a lilac gauze overskirt; its matching kitten-heeled slippers bore diamond buckles cunningly shaped as primroses. Once eaten by the Monster, Mariamoni would no longer think of ball gowns.

She closed her eyes and listened to the wild voice of the sea.

"Hey!"

Mariamoni's eyes snapped open. A human voice or a gull's cry?

Behind her, leather scraped on rock and a light tenor voice cursed. She rolled her head to the other side and beheld a slender figure clad in shirt, pants, and boots: not a priest. His light hair had been cropped close to his elegant skull; it glowed in the torchlight. A silver pin with a huge cabochon stone reflected light at his collar. When his second leg swung on top of the rock, he hauled up things that clanked.

Mariamoni looked beyond his clothing for the first time and said, without quite meaning to do so, "How *old* are you?" His skin, pale as milk, completely lacked beard.

He looked at her sidelong and said, "Old enough to rescue you." The hilt of a broadsword poked up above his shoulder, worn in a harness across his back; the weapon's immense size made him seem even younger. Mariamoni looked in vain for the hammer and chisel she was sure he must have brought to cleave her manacles.

"Don't look so worried, I have plenty of weapons," he said, and sat cross-legged next to Mariamoni's head. Something in the lithe shifting of his body, the jut of his hips—

Mariamoni gasped. "You're a woman!"

She smiled, showing many teeth. "If you don't like that, I can—"

"Don't you dare! Let me go!"

"Can't do that yet, Princess. You are a princess?"

Mariamoni said, "My uncle would have the country believe

otherwise, but yes, I am the Princess Mariamoni."

"My name is Trude. I'll split the pearls with you."

Trude must be crazed, Mariamoni thought. Crazed to come here, crazed to talk about mysterious jewels. Could she believe anything this woman told her? She said, as calmly as she could, "I would be pleased to accept nothing more than the release of my bonds." She attempted to elegantly lift one wrist, but was chained too tightly. Her wrist rebounded, and the manacle clanked against the stone.

Trude laughed. "The Monster won't come if you aren't chained up." She withdrew a flask from her bag and held it to Mariamoni's lips: cool, fresh water.

Humor her, Mariamoni thought, trying not to gulp the water in an unladylike fashion. *Humor her.*

Trude stopped laughing, leaned forward and brushed hair off Mariamoni's cheek. "It won't eat you—I'm going to kill it for the pearls."

Mariamoni had been through too many emotional extremes this day. She simply couldn't follow. Trude's callused fingers on her cheek felt better than the finest silken chemise. She wondered what was wrong with her, that she could both distrust and relax simultaneously. Perhaps her situation contributed, but she was intrigued despite her fear. She closed her eyes. "Please explain this to me slowly. I am afraid I do not quite understand."

The hand left her cheek. Bereft, she opened her eyes and found Trude's face much closer than it had been before. Trude leaned down and firmly pressed her lips to Mariamoni's, held for a moment, and retreated. The tingle from that touch took several breaths to pass through Mariamoni's body down to her toes. Trude watched her solemnly. Mariamoni licked her lips and said, "That was not an explanation, but I must admit I found it quite pleasant."

Trude grinned. She said, "Don't be worried. The Monster always comes at dawn, but you'll be safe. It can only eat you if your lips have never been kissed."

"That's an old wives' tale, I'm afraid. Ranta the Bouncing Tavern Maid, of local fame, attempted that safety but was eaten posthaste."

Trude said, "Ranta the Bouncing Tavern Maid didn't have the details right. I'll bet she had lips that had never been kissed. Men are such clods. I bet you do, too."

"You kissed me only moments ago," Mariamoni pointed out, "and I have had beaux before." Slobbering, annoying beaux who wore too much velvet, but she did not say that.

"Your *other* lips."

"Oth—oh!" Mariamoni's cheeks flamed beneath her sunburn. One did not mention one's nether parts. One did not think of that place or touch there or even wash there: that was for bath maids to take care of, and even they only washed royalty through a concealing layer of thick cotton gloves. Mariamoni wondered what it would be like to have Trude bathe her. She envisioned the other woman's cropped hair damp and clinging to her forehead from steam, her cheekbones flushed pink as carnations, her slim body draped in a pale green shift brocaded with droplets and adhering damply to the slight curve of her bosom.

Trude grinned again. Her smile engendered a strange hollowness in Mariamoni's abdomen and weakened her limbs. Trude said, "I'll make you safe, then when the Monster comes at dawn, I'll kill it. Its crop is full of black pearls. We take the pearls and go overland to Port Cazziopiya and take ship for the East. That would be impossible without money, so you see the danger is necessary."

In Trude's matter-of-fact tones, the plan sounded eminently

practical and wise. Not only would she be alive and in the company of a fascinating individual, but she could purchase many fabulous fabrics in the East. Mariamoni said, "As you have probably guessed, I *do* need your help. If I'd escaped this rock on my own, I would have had no idea how to go on. I will be pleased to accompany you."

"Good."

"But I should like to know who you are."

"A rogue of no home. My cousin wanted to marry me to some drooling old man to recoup his finances. This was after he took my father's earldom from me, simply because I have no dangly bits."

"Dangly bits." Mariamoni flushed again. "Ahem." She studied Trude in silence for a while. The sun glinted off her hair, russet as a fox's pelt. Her cinnamon eyes were adorned by thick, curling lashes the warm, rutilant hue of a forest deer's flank. Despite the calluses, her hands had a slender elegance that could not come from hard labor; she could well believe Trude had noble blood. Corseted, dressed in a gown, her hair long, a touch of color to highlight her prominent cheekbones, and she would be lovely, especially with those eyes.

Mariamoni was faintly disturbed to find Trude lovely even without those necessary elaborations. Perhaps men would prefer a more abundant bosom, but Mariamoni thought that, considered with the rest of her form, which was flexible as a sapling, her gentle curves were really quite pleasing. The male clothing accentuated her shape and complemented her forthright behavior. The idea of kissing Trude again prickled over her skin, much like the stinging, salty breeze.

The air felt distinctly cooler now, especially in her damp dress. Mariamoni's nipples budded to hard, painful points that rasped the silk lining of her bust improver. She said, "I acquiesce."

Trude bent closer, then shifted back and removed her dagger from its hip sheath. Mariamoni shivered, not entirely from cold. She couldn't believe what was about to happen, yet at the same time, it seemed inevitable as the sun.

"Are-are you sure you can kill the Monster?"

Trude said, not boasting, "I've killed buck and boar, and once my father and I killed a mountain cat that had turned man-eater."

"The Monster's neck is as tall as three horses."

"The seamen I talked with said the Monster breathes water, so when it comes into the air it's slower and clumsier. They told me exactly where to strike." As she spoke, she slipped free loops and buckles, finally laying her sheathed blade near to hand. Freed of the harness, her shape was unmistakably womanly; Mariamoni couldn't think how she'd missed it before.

Trude stretched, arching her back, before kneeling next to Mariamoni and bending close. "You're not scared, are you?"

"Not in the least." A princess didn't prevaricate...except to protect her dignity. Spread-eagled as she was, Mariamoni felt exposed despite her several layers of proper clothing. If she looked down, she could see her bosom jutting upward; cool air wafted beneath the hem of her skirt.

Confidently, Trude said, "I'll protect you," and leaned down for a kiss, this time flicking Mariamoni's lips with her tongue. But it was not at all disagreeable, not at all like the sloppy, dog-like licks of Prince Jurard.

"I thought—I thought you said that would be of no use in this circumstance."

"No, but I like it."

"Oh."

"Much nicer than kissing the Baron Ralntyn."

"I'm so glad," Mariamoni said, warmed by sudden fellow

feeling. "It would be quite all right with me if you did that again." She licked her dry lips and smiled.

Trude's mouth came down on hers, wide and wet and warm. She sucked at Mariamoni's lips as if they were small candies in the flavor she desired above all others. Mariamoni had never realized how slick and hot the interior of a mouth could be, nor how sweet. Now that she had been reminded of her nether lips, she found she could not ignore them; even without direct stimulation, they grew disproportionately large in her awareness, tender and slippery. She tugged restlessly at her bonds.

Trude gradually shifted position, bringing their bodies closer together. Mariamoni welcomed her warmth and weight, especially the pressure against her bosom, which created a certain deep, pleasurable ache. Her limbs ached, too, with yearning to wrap herself around Trude, a yearning that could not be satisfied. Every futile movement against her bonds intensified her distress. In her mind, she screamed for more, more, more. The rock beneath her bottom, so unforgiving earlier, now seemed a necessary solidity against which to press.

Trude's mouth descended again, this time to suck upon Mariamoni's neck, the most delicious sensation she had yet experienced. Trude could devour her and she would not care, so long as she sucked Mariamoni's flesh into her mouth like that, just like that. An involuntary exclamation escaped her, then another.

"You taste like flowers," Trude said, her voice darker, rougher than before. "Flowers here...and here..."

"Ah-att-attar of oh-orchid," Mariamoni gasped. Trude was squeezing her breast, a completely impossible liberty that she never wanted to end.

Trude smelled mostly of leather and horses, and sweet cardamom she must have used on her hair. Mariamoni arched upward. She wanted to throw her arms about Trude so badly she nearly screamed her frustration like a common fishwife.

Trude seemed to share her feelings. "Be damned, I didn't think it would be like this!"

"More," Mariamoni demanded. "It hurts. Put your hand there." She indicated with her chin.

Trude lifted up slightly. "Oh, there," she said, grinning and panting at the same time.

Mariamoni wanted to scream out a vast babble of commands and pleas and warnings and whimpers. She bit her lip. "Please."

"Glad to, Your Highness." Trude gathered up handfuls of Mariamoni's skirt and pushed it upward.

The fabric was already ruined, so Mariamoni steeled herself against the additional crushing, surprised to find she wanted Trude to proceed more quickly. She felt as if she was boiling from within. Beneath her lace unmentionables, her heat felt wetter than the sea.

Her skirts and petticoats made such a mound at her waist that Mariamoni could no longer see Trude, but she felt her unmentionables being untied and eased down over her thighs. Her desperation had eased a fraction once Trude took action. A whisper of breeze brushed her bare skin and she shivered. To compose herself, Mariamoni tilted her head back and contemplated the sky's rapidly deepening blue as Trude slid her hands deliciously up from Mariamoni's knees, running her callused hands delicately over skin that only Mariamoni and her bath maids had ever touched before. This was nothing like the impersonal handling of a bath maid, and unlike her own touch, she could not predict the wonderful tingling warmth of Trude's hands. "More, please," she said.

Mariamoni felt warm breath on her skin, like a feather brushing along her nerves. She thought she would die with the

waiting, yet at the same time could imagine nothing more wonderful than this breathless state between her old life and a new
one of bravery and adventure.

She found she was wrong when wet heat pressed against her
lower lips, and Trude's tongue, for the merest instant, flicked
inside her very body. Mariamoni tried to speak, to express her
wonder, but only a choked sound escaped.

Trude stopped.

"No! Do that again!" Mariamoni commanded.

"You taste good," Trude said.

"I *am* a princess," Mariamoni reminded her. Regretting her
outburst of a moment before, she added, "Please, do go on. That
was the very best kiss I have ever experienced."

Trude's head appeared above the pile of skirts, rather like a
puppet from its stage. "Women should taste good; they're so
much softer and rounder than men. Like fresh rolls are better
than an old, stale loaf."

Mariamoni was about to express her approbation for this phi-
losophizing when Trude bent back to her task. She speedily lost
herself in the delicate sensations of Trude's tongue manipulating
her nether lips like fingers on harp strings, producing shimmers
of sensation that built to some unknowable crescendo. A momentary thought of the Monster to come chilled her, until an
unexpected spear of pleasure nearly stopped her heart. Her lower
body shuddered, but somehow not quite deeply enough. Her nipples scraped against cloth and she wanted Trude to touch them,
touch all of her, but not stop what she was doing now, either.

Mariamoni must have made some noise, for Trude proceeded
with more vigor, reaching one hand around the pile of skirts to
brush over the embroidered panel covering Mariamoni's abdomen, fumbling and then pressing as if trying to achieve a steady-
ing grip. Trude's mouth suckled as if eating a warm, ripe peach

swollen with thick, sweet juice. Mariamoni felt as if her body were being drawn into Trude's mouth and there twisted, too tightly, even more tightly than that, until she snapped, weeping gently with the relief of it. Her tears slid across her cheeks and wetness tracked down her thighs, not blood but something whose musky, salty scent drifted to her nostrils like the sea breeze.

Afterward, she remembered how cold and wet and filthy she was, and would have wept again with exhaustion and fear had Trude not lain beside her, nearly covering her smaller form with her solid, leather-scented length; her legs nestled between Mariamoni's thighs as if to protect her tender center, still throbbing amid the languid slackness of her muscles and thoughts.

Mariamoni savored Trude's cheek brushing hers, the soft pressure against her left breast, and the scent of leather, enveloping her in safety and warmth.

Light woke her, and Trude's absence. She whipped her head from side to side, seeking. Strands of hair blew over her face from the movement and from a fishy gust of cool air that sent fear spasming down her spine.

Then she saw the Monster.

A small, round head swept toward her, the termination of a long, snakelike neck with skin brighter than gold coins. Its mouth gaped, revealing teeth like a dense forest of tiny daggers jutting forward and back as if too many for even a Monster's maw to contain. Its head loomed closer, closer, and its huge nostril-shaped gills flared and fluttered, sucking in her scent. Her shriek vanished under its roar.

Abruptly, its mouth snapped shut on empty air, and it reared back.

Trude's boot landed near Mariamoni's ear, skidding in the slime. Mariamoni glimpsed a flash of silver—the boar spear plunging toward the Monster's throat. It struck. Cool, viscous liquid sprayed. Mariamoni choked and gagged. Trude shouted. The Monster's roar gargled, and more ichor gushed interminably, over Mariamoni, over Trude, and over the rock.

A heavy weight thudded on Mariamoni's bosom, driving the air from her lungs. Gasping and sputtering, she tried to open her eyes, but they were glued shut by the Monster's foul blood.

Trude heaved away the Monster's head. She produced a hammer and chisel, clanged them against Mariamoni's bonds—suddenly, she was free. Mariamoni immediately curled her stiff body together, scrubbing her face against her once-lovely frock.

She heard a meaty *thunk*, then a horrid wet squishing sound. Trude crowed, "We're rich!" She flung her arms around Mariamoni, clutching her tightly and spilling moist pearls into her lap. Mariamoni began to laugh.

Once clean and properly dressed, she felt sure she would be ecstatic. For now, she leaned into Trude's embrace and gratefully returned it, glad just to be alive.

She would buy a new gown to celebrate.

DOWN THE BASEMENT

Ryan Field

One Halloween night during my senior year in college, I went to a costume party in a broken-down frat house, dressed as a character I'd been inventing for months—years, if you really want to get technical. I looked like any normal guy in college by then: short, sandy blond hair, blue eyes, white polo shirts, and khaki slacks. Though I was only five feet, six inches tall, there was nothing about me on the outside you would have considered peculiar. Most people would never have guessed that I was gay or that I had a secret passion for lipstick, earrings, and very high heels.

It's not that I didn't like being a man; I did and wouldn't have changed that for the world. But the thought of shaving my entire body to the point where every conceivable inch of skin was smooth and soft, and then putting on a tight corset, black stockings, and dangerous stilettos gave me an erection that lasted for hours. Good sex for me was all about dressing up. All this was only fantasy, and though I'd once had the courage to buy a pair of cheap, size-eleven, four-inch heels at Payless (buried at the bottom of my suitcase and only worn while I masturbated in private), I'd never actually had the guts to go out in public dressed as a slutty woman.

Not until the night of the costume party, anyway. I wasn't cruising for guys, either; I just wanted to dress up and feel sexy for once. I'd spent months ordering the most precise items on the Internet, things I knew would make me appear and feel really hot. The general costume consisted of a black, beaded evening bag, a short, black taffeta skirt, a skin-tight, black lace corset trimmed in silver, a black mask that covered half my face, and six-inch black stilettos. But it was the small details that really made the costume work: rhinestone earrings, necklace and bracelet, long, red fake fingernails, full makeup, and a pair of realistic vinyl boobs, with big nipples, that felt real when you squeezed them. I'd signed up at a tanning salon a month before the party so my legs would be smooth and brown…no need for stockings. And, best of all, a long blond wig with a snug fit so I could toss my head around without worrying about losing it.

Actually, my only real worry was holding my eight-inch penis down all night. I found a strong black thong-sock (no string, so my ass would be bare) with a heavy waistband to keep things concealed. I knew if I got really hard I could point my dick toward my stomach and the waistband would hold it down. Though I made a few mistakes (didn't need eye makeup with a mask…when the wig was on my head I realized all I needed was a little red lip gloss to pass), my first time going out in public was quite professional. And it was *supposed* to be outrageous; this was a costume party, after all.

The high heels made me feel sexual and powerful, and as I strutted across campus to the frat house party, a couple of

guys turned to stare at my bare legs. They weren't the best-look-
ing boys on campus, but they were real men—they were pussy
hounds and they liked the way I looked. I concentrated very
carefully on my movements so that I wouldn't appear masculine.
I didn't want to come off as quasi feminine, either, so I simply
restricted each movement to avoid anything awkward or too
calculated. Then I smiled and said, "Hey, guys." The tall dude,
a horny African-American, said, "Yeah, sweet baby, where you
been all my life?"

I told him, "Going to meet my boyfriend, sweetie." He
laughed, and while I continued to walk away, I heard him tell
his friend, "I'd like to get me a piece of that sugar, man. I know
how to make her happy." If I'd had any doubts about being able
to pass as a woman, those two boys proved I could do it as long
as I was careful.

The costume was a huge hit, and no one recognized me or
even considered I might not be a woman. No one from my usual
crowd was there, anyway; I was an English major, and those
people were all jocks and cheerleaders. I was glad I'd worn the
sock underwear; my dick was semi-erect the entire time, especially when I realized that young guys were staring at my legs.
But the goal was to have fun passing as a woman for the first
time, nothing more. And, if for some reason I was recognized
by anyone, I knew I could camp it up as a man in drag, just an
outrageous Halloween costume for fun.

Some of the other costumes were good, too: A kinky witch
(I think she was a real woman) with big boobs in black leather and lace, a scarecrow who was actually smoking from the
shoulders, one really swishy gay guy dressed as Baby Jane Hudson, and a guy with a realistic Richard Nixon mask are a few
that still come to mind. But others weren't all that creative, l
ike the humpy guys with deep voices who didn't bother to come

up with a real costume and just wore their football uniforms with black masks.

It turned out to be one of those parties where you don't really have to know anyone very well to have a good time, and because it was a costume party people seemed more animated behind their masks. I laughed and joked with Baby Jane Hudson, while Richard Nixon kept bringing me strong drinks and trying to put his hand up my little black skirt. At one point, with the palm of his hand pressed against my ass, he leaned over and whispered, "My car is parked outside."

And I replied, "Sorry, stud, I have a boyfriend." He was cool about it and didn't persist. I would have loved to at least given him a blow job, only I was terrified he'd find out who I really was and kick my ass.

We all partied hard, mixing beer and whatever else there was, all night long. Sometime around two in the morning, one of the drunken football players reached behind me while I was leaning against a wide oak staircase and placed the palm of his large hand up my skirt and rested it on my bare ass. His pale blue eyes appeared eager; one eyebrow rose for the conquest. He squeezed my ass cheeks and said, "Those fucking high heels are really hot." He was about six four, and towered over me in spite of the stilettos; his words were slurred and his breath heavy and stale from beer when he asked, "Why aren't you wearing any underwear?"

"So you can put your hand up my dress, sweetie, and feel my ass." I couldn't believe my own words, but there, I'd said it.

He then asked if I wanted to go down to the basement recreation room, to smoke a joint with three of his football buddies. I agreed, and he nodded to his three buddies who must have been waiting for a signal. He led me downstairs with his large hand pressed against the small of my back as though I belonged to him.

The basement was dark, with just two dim light bulbs with pull strings, and I had to navigate with care because of the high heels. A dusty old braided rug had been placed in the center of the concrete floor; my heels sank into the grooves. A large sectional sofa with worn navy fabric and a square, dark pine coffee table with heavy, turned legs rested upon the stained rug. The football player told me, "Have a seat, baby," while he pulled a small bag from beneath a sofa cushion and proceeded to roll a joint on the coffee table. I put the black evening bag on the coffee table, sat in the middle of the sofa, and crossed my legs like a lady. A moment later, I heard the sound of heavy footsteps clomping down the stairs—his three football buddies, I assumed. Though I had to clench my fists to keep them from shaking, the thought of three strong football players with big floppy dicks who were all hot for me caused my ass to literally twitch.

They were so drunk they couldn't stand straight. They were joking and laughing and shoving each other around playfully, saying things in deep voices like, "Get the fuck out of here, dude," and, "Fuck, yeah, man, you pussy." Bad little locker room boys with too much testosterone, having too much fun at a party in front of a slutty young girl who was showing too much leg that night. One still held a bottle of vodka in his right hand. I knew none of them would ask me to the senior prom, but I also knew they wanted to get into my pants in the worst way. Though I'd been drinking, I was far from drunk and calculated my every move very carefully. I knew if they found out they'd beat me to a pulp, and by then it was too late to leave them gracefully.

"C'mon over here and sit on my lap, so I can take off that mask," said the football player who'd brought me down to the basement. He'd removed his mask by then and was smoking the joint, about to pass it to one of his buddies.

Two of them sat down on my right, the third on my left. They were quiet by then, but their eyes were eager and their expressions blank, not sure who would make the first move. None were wearing masks; they'd probably gotten hot and lost them upstairs somewhere.

I smiled. "I want to smoke first." I leaned over, pressed my palm on the upper thigh of the guy next to me, while he held the joint and I took a long drag. I knew if we all got stoned and they got so wasted they didn't know what day of the week it was, I wouldn't have to worry about being discovered.

The one who wanted me on his lap, the leader of the pack, stood and walked over to a bookcase where there was a large television and one of those small Bose radios. He turned on the radio and turned up the volume, and Mary K. Blige began to sing. "Let's dance," he said, grabbing my hand and pulling me off the sofa.

The other three, still passing the joint around, howled, "Go man, yeah, look at her move."

I fell into his strapping body and placed my arms around his wide shoulders. He pulled me closer, and then put his rough hands under my dress and lifted it all the way up to my waist so the other guys could see him petting my bare ass. We began to dance very slowly; I arched my back and invited him to play with my ass cheeks while I rubbed the back of his thick neck. His breath smelled like pot and beer; I slowly licked the stubble below his ear, and he moaned. One of the guys on the sofa, a tall, lanky dude with huge hands, stood and staggered up behind me. He put his hands around my waist, shoved his crotch against my ass and began to slowly hump his erection, banging against the crack of my ass. I reached down with my right hand and began to massage the one in front, an erection so hard and thick I felt it pulse through the fabric of his football pants. He leaned forward and stuck his tongue in my mouth while the one behind me reached down and began to gently squeeze my ass.

I knew I had to change course; the next drunken move would be to reach between my legs for a pussy that wasn't there. So I untangled myself from the sandwich and said, "Okay, boys, everyone on the sofa."

They were eager to please; the joint was finished, and they were all too wasted to remember anything by that point. The leader, who'd brought me down there in the first place, sat off to the side at the edge of the sofa and watched; the other three sat next to each other. I slowly went down on my knees and began to unlace the football pants of the one who had been behind me dancing. I pulled his pants down to his knees; a nine-inch erection popped out because he wasn't wearing underwear. I then removed his shoes and pulled his pants off altogether. While he moaned, and the others grabbed their crotches, I ran my long red fingernails up his dark hairy legs, took hold of the erection and began to slurp and suck as though I hadn't been fed dick in years. He tasted salty and smelled like vinegar and cheese because his balls had been sweating during the party. With my dark-red lips wrapped around the head, I began to jerk the shaft with my right hand. He blew a load into my mouth within minutes, and I gulped the whole thing and sucked out the last drops so there wouldn't be any mess.

I wasted no time in repeating the same act with the guy sitting next to him, which took even less time (horny, drunk boys get off fast, I learned). But when I reached the third, who had already pulled his dick out for me, the leader at the edge of the sofa leaned over and whispered, "I want to fuck you, baby."

My eyes bugged as though I'd been caught with my hand in the cookie jar, and he seemed to sense the fear.

"Don't worry," he whispered, "I know you're not a girl. I

knew it when I asked you to go down the basement. I just wanna fuck you, please."

"But what about him?" Though the first two were already snoring; the third guy with heavy, glazed eyes waited for his blow job, too. His dick stood from the opening of the football pants, and he was jerking off. He was slightly overweight (the linebacker type) but had really sexy, sloppy bull-sized balls I couldn't wait to lick.

"Just get up, lean over the arm of the sofa, and spread your legs," he said. "You can suck him off while I bang you. I know you want it."

We both stood, while the last guy watched as though he couldn't predict what would happen next, and I leaned over the arm of the sofa and wrapped my red lips around the head of his cock. He didn't care what would happen after that; he only wanted to get sucked off so he could go to sleep, too. His dick was curved and long—not as thick as the first guy and not as sweet as the second, but I couldn't help liking the way it hit the back of my throat when I sucked all the way down to his sour ball sac. Oddly enough, it occurred to me that I was even more turned on now that the leader knew I was really a guy.

While I sucked the third guy off, the leader pulled his fat cock out, lifted my black taffeta skirt up to my waist and spread my ass cheeks. He blew a huge wad of spit; it hit my hole and he pressed the head of his dick against it. He rolled the head around for a moment to lube me and then slowly inserted the tip. I arched my back and spread my legs; he grabbed my knees and lifted them with both hands so that he could pound away. With my legs bent at the knees and high heels in the air, he fucked like a machine, and I moaned and continued to suck off the football player on the sofa. The harder the one behind me hammered, the harder I sucked the cock in my mouth.

Again, it didn't take long for either of them to reach climax. But something happened to me, too, that I hadn't expected. The one behind me began to hit a sensitive spot, and my orgasm began to rise. And as the guy on the sofa grabbed the back of my blond wig to let me know he was coming, the one behind me blew his load up my hole, and I shot my load into the black thong. While I slurped up and swallowed the last drops from guy number three, and the leader was still depositing his last drops of seed up my ass, I couldn't believe I'd had an orgasm without touching myself. He remained inside for a few moments while I gently licked the third guy's sloppy ball sac.

Then he pulled out fast, helped me to my feet, and offered another drink. The other three were now passed out and snoring. The minute I started to lick and suck the third guy's balls he began to snore.

"Why not," I said, taking a couple of long swigs from a bottle of vodka. He put his arm around my waist and pulled me to his chest, drops of him now trickling down my bare legs...the room began to spin.

"You certainly do deserve it," said the leader. "You worked hard tonight."

I smiled, but nearly lost my balance; the last drink of vodka had now put me over the edge, too. "You were wonderful. You made me come without touching my dick." I reached down and cupped his dick and balls in my hand.

"You have a great hole, baby," he said

I passed out right after that and don't remember anything until I woke up about three hours later, face down across two snoring football players who wore nothing but jock straps; one great athletic hand was resting on the middle of my ass...my face pressed to the crook of a hairy sack of balls. Though I did take a couple of quick sniffs, and the tip of my tongue couldn't help licking the guy's tangy ball sac for a few minutes, I suddenly became terrified they would wake up and beat the shit out of me. I slowly rose, while the guys continued to snore, and searched for my black beaded bag. The basement was dark; I couldn't find it anywhere.

A deep football player voice said, "Looking for this?" His eyes were heavy as he waved my bag in the air.

"Ah, yes," I said, still trying to remember everything that had happened that night.

He handed me the bag. "No kiss good-bye?"

I looked at him and smirked. I'd just remembered he was the kinky boy who knew I wasn't a woman. "Why didn't you beat the shit out of me last night?"

"They really thought you were a girl, and I'm into it—chicks with dicks," he said, trying hard to speak clearly. "Last night was really hot, man...maybe we could hook up again sometime, just you and me."

I reached into my bag, pulled out a card with my e-mail address and handed it to him. "But the ball is in your court, buddy," I said. "This could be a once-in-a-lifetime thing for me. I don't usually do this, and I'm not sure I ever will again. Just wanted to have a little fun on Halloween."

He smiled and then put his hand up my dress. "I'll get in touch and this can be our little secret. But next time I want to see you in red high heels with a red garter belt."

I leaned forward and kissed him good-bye. He put his hand up my dress one more time, and then I quietly left while the football players were still sleeping.

SOME THINGS NEVER CHANGE

Melinda Johnson

Writing is a lonely profession, so I break the monotony sometimes by doing a little drag. I'm not the world's greatest drag king, but still, there's nothing like the feeling you get from prancing around on stage, women whistling and screaming for you. But it's more than that, really. I love the way a drag king or queen can be old, saggy, butt-ugly in either gender, but what counts is that they're up there, doing it. The shows I do are very small, in an old, beat-up hall on the east side of town, but when I'm up there, I feel like I'm king of the world. I even throw a few Leo references into my act sometimes, just to amuse myself. No true drag artist can resist a pun. It's that magic, the magic of the stage, that lets awkward, geeky me get a few girls now and then. Like Christine.

I can replay my first sight of her like a movie in my head. The MC, Mr. Dick Manly, resplendent in a blue sequined tux, had just announced me, "Put your hands together, ladies, for that stud muffin, Herman Leman!" My music started, and I strutted slowly on stage, keeping time to a slow, throbbing electronic beat. I don't dance so much as pose, gesture languidly, and gradually peel off my outfit. I make a pretty convincing guy, as long as I strap down my generous chest and add a little judicial facial hair. I've been told I look a lot like a female James Dean—the same cast of face, the same carriage. Well, maybe James Dean after a nice motherly type fed him up properly; I've always been stocky and I capitalize on it by lifting weights.

I was dressed in black pants, black shirt, black leather jacket. I walked out on stage, hands on hips. The crowd whistled. And I saw her. They must have seen my tongue hit the floor from the back row. She was a small, slim woman dressed to kill in an acid-green sequined dress and a hot-pink feather boa. Both were Value Village specials and showed some wear on closer inspection, but from my view on the stage, she shone like a scarlet rhododendron gleaming through the mists of a soft Vancouver rain. I stood open-mouthed, staring, missed my cue to start flexing.

"Whatsa matter? Never seen a room full of girls before?" some heckler yelled. That brought me back.

"I've never seen a room filled with girls this hot. I was blinded by the splendor," I yelled, slipping back into character. "In fact, you are all sooooo hot," I grabbed the edges of my jacket and glowered, "I gotta take my jacket off." Then I started my act. I shed my leather jacket, struck a few poses. Slowly unbuttoned and slid off my black satin shirt, revealing a black tank top. More poses. All the while drooling after the girl in green. Gyrated my pelvis a few times, grabbed my amply stuffed crotch. Always good for a few catcalls.

I turned around, wiggled my ass for them, flexed my arms, and slowly peeled off my black tank top—not an easy job, since it was reinforced with industrial-strength elastic to keep my breasts squished down. I turned, revealing my chest covered in a black leather bra. I glanced down, opened my mouth in shock at seeing breasts. Then I grinned in appreciation of them, an appreciation I feel they deserve. I squeezed them a few times, looking the girl in green straight in the eyes, picturing her hands pinching my nipples. The mental image of her hands on my breasts nearly caused my knees to buckle. I ran my hands down my sides, loving the cheers and applause, turned around again, shook my ass, and ripped off my pants.

I wore black leather short shorts, and they bulged visibly when I turned around. I slowly slid my hand into my crotch, wet as always from the stares of the crowd. I rooted around in there for a minute, looking my dream girl straight in the eye, then I pulled out a lollipop, gave it a slow lick, and strutted off the stage with as much dignity and swagger as I could muster. Even if I do say so myself, it was the finest performance of my drag career, fueled as it was by searing lust and a desperate attempt to seduce the mystery woman through my irresistible charm. At least, that's what I tell myself.

Backstage, I collapsed against the grungy wall. Dick, who never missed a beat, or a beating, was grinning at me like the Cheshire Cat. I grabbed a handful of Dick's shiny blue lapel. "Dick," I said, "she got me. Straight through the heart. A fatal blow." I slumped down, clutched my chest. "I'm just gonna sit here an' slowly fade away."

"No," he grabbed me, hauled me up, surprisingly strong for such a slight woman, and hissed, "you're going to take your bow, and then you're going to talk to her."

"Talk to her?" I squeaked, before I was pushed out to take a bow. Dick, otherwise known as Sondra, a legal assistant who goes to her day job in miniskirts and pantyhose, was a close friend of mine, and she was in on the secret. I'm shy. Hopelessly, helplessly shy. Performing is easy for me, but to actually talk to a woman? A person I don't know? Eek. Not going to happen.

But, miraculously, it did. Christine isn't as shy as I am. Once the chairs had been cleared away and the dance music started, I ventured out onto the floor, still in my leather bra, still packing a sizable bulge, but having added pants. I saw Christine looking at me. I took a deep breath, and, drawing my Herman persona around me like a cape, I gave her my best hello-lady-don't-you-look-fine smile. For the first time, it actually worked. She came straight over to me and took the reins of the courtship ritual into her own very capable hands. I found out how capable a little later when she dragged me out into the back alley and swarmed over me, hands everywhere, kissing me with an intensity that made me gasp.

We leaned against the rough wall, a Dumpster to the right of us, the chill air bringing up goose bumps on our sweaty bodies. Her red lacquered nails found my nipples, pinched them the way I'd dreamed on stage she would. I stroked her finely muscled back, buried my fingers in her long, sweet-smelling chestnut hair. I was lost in amazement at the feel of her body, her dancer's body, rippling with muscle yet supple, lithe, boneless.

Despite her beauty, her perfection, I focused on the small flaws. Those are my favorite parts; they always have been. Her arms were covered with freckles, and she had a small scab on her right arm that my fingers caught on as I stroked her. I could see the spot on her nose where she had taken out a nose ring, and her left earlobe had a beauty mark on it that looked like a tiny jet earring from a distance. As eager as I was to caress her, know her, merge with her, time seemed to slow for me as I explored these little details. It was those small things that made her real, separated her from the smooth-and-creamy dream girls I slept with each night.

I sucked her earlobe into my mouth, tasting the bitterness of the perfume she'd dabbed behind her ear and the clean, fresh taste of her skin. She moaned as I stuck my tongue into her ear, bit gently on her lobe. I could feel her sink into my arms and I tightened my grasp on her. Finally, she climbed on me, wrapping her legs around me as I held her, leaning back against the rough wall for support, my cunt throbbing as she rode the dildo I wore, each stroke driving the base of it against my clit, until we came together, moaning desperately. I was shaking so much I almost dropped her.

We leaned against the wall, panting. Just then, I heard a crash and a cat's howl.

"Yikes!" I squealed, jumping, my dildo bobbing wildly. Christine doubled over laughing, and my ability to look tough, cool, and dignified in front of her was forever ruined.

We went home together that night, and we've spent almost every night together since. Our second anniversary is just a few weeks away.

Christine is a tremendous gift to me. She brought me out of myself. I had always been shy, afraid to talk to strangers. She helped me unfold. She is high femme, glamorous, and beautiful, and she moves through the world with an inborn social knowledge that leaves me in awe.

And she's a flirt, a terrible flirt. More than once, I have been tempted to pull an old-school butch act on some hapless woman and haul her out the back door and black her eyes for talking to my girl. Of course, I'd never do it. I'm a pacifist. Besides, it's always Christine's fault, anyway, the incorrigible flirt. Not to mention that we always have hotter sex after one of her "conquests." She'll tease me about how cute the other woman was, tell me all the things she wanted to do to her, until I rip her clothes off, do everything she described, desperate to show her with my hands and tongue and devotion that no one can please her like I can.

Not that it's been smooth sailing the whole time. We're both difficult people in our own ways, and we've each taken refuge on a friend's couch a few times. Fortunately, we both have a sense of humor. For example, a few months after we moved in together, we almost came to blows over whose stuff went where and who was supposed to clean the place. It got so tense I spent the weekend at Dick's. When I got back, there was nothing in the apartment but our bed, the computer, and a Zen print. Christine was sitting on the floor, meditating. I nearly passed out in shock, until she told me that all our stuff was in the storage locker. Then I found it funny. We moved some stuff back, tossed other crap, and made it work.

My Chris is so beautiful to me. Her slight dancer's body, so slender and delicate yet rippling with strength, takes my breath away. She fills me with feelings of gallantry. I want to open doors for her, carry her packages. If we were in school, I'd beg to carry her books. Walking down the street with her, I feel huge, powerful, hulking over her finely made body. Even though I have the more feminine body, all big tits and full hips, while Christine is boyishly slim, the sleek green gown she'd worn when I first met her formed my mental picture of her. Despite her swearing and nasty talk and drawer full of restraints, I see her as a lady. My awe of her womanhood, my need to cherish her, had started more than a few arguments; Christine has a rabid feminist streak in her.

"I can carry my own packages, you know!" She'd yelled at me one day as we walked down Commercial Drive, the funky once-Italian neighborhood that had been overrun by hippies and dykes. I'd wrested her grocery bags away from her, trying to be a gentleman, and somehow I irritated her sense of independence. "I'm strong!" she glowered at me. "See! Can you do this?" She gracefully flipped onto her hands, right there in the middle of the street, and slowly raised her right arm in the air, balancing only on her left. Soft clapping and a few wolf whistles reached us from the drooling dykes sipping their cappuccinos in the coffee shop next to us. Her skirt had fallen around her waist, revealing her loose boxers, covered in smiling cats—her "happy pussy panties," as she called them. Christine flipped upright, her movements as fluid as mercury.

"I certainly can't. But I can do this!" Still holding her shopping bags, I bent down and scooped her up into my arms, *An Officer and a Gentleman* style, and marched triumphantly down the street toward our shabby apartment. Her indignation gave way to delight, and she kissed me, deeply. But the issue wasn't over. Later that night, after we'd had sex on the kitchen table where I'd dumped her and the grocery bags, my exhausted arms shaking so much I could barely cradle her head in my hands while I kissed her, she brought up the issue again.

"Al, Allie, Alyssa, my baby," she whispered, stroking my cheek, her naming of me a brief history in reverse of my search for identity, "why must you always pose like that?" Her blue eyes looked deep into mine. "It's cute sometimes, but at others, it gets to be a little much. I'm not a fragile princess, needing a white knight to save her. I'm a big girl. I can open my own car doors, carry my own packages. I don't want or need a protector. It's fun to dress up in an evening gown, do my makeup, and walk out in my heels, take your arm with you in your forties gangster suit. But that's just play, you silly woman. I just want you. Not an act, not your wardrobe—you. All that good stuff that's in you, like the chocolate under the M&M's crunchy shell."

A lump rose in my throat as she spoke, at the thought of how well she knew me, how well she could look into my heart, despite the fact that I could rarely articulate how I felt. I wrote her stories, instead—poems, limericks, anything—hiding my true self under the handy guise of narrator, a role I felt comfortable with. But she could look beneath that, to the human under the role. And I loved her for it.

"But," I tried to speak, had to clear my throat to continue, "don't you get it? Sometimes the princess is saving the white knight. It's she who tells him who he is, you see." I looked down and to the side, unable to meet her bright blue eyes. Even after all this time, I still couldn't meet her eyes when I spoke about my feelings. I gripped her cool, soft hand, tried to articulate how I felt.

"You see, when I was a kid, a teenager, I was lost. I didn't belong. I didn't know who I was. Then, when I came here, I started going to dyke bars; I fell in love with butches. I wanted to be like them. I wanted their attitude. I saw what I wanted to become." I half-smiled at her, glanced up at her eyes. "There's just something about butches, the way they carry themselves, hold themselves. The way a woman who is pug-ugly by straight standards can dress butch, act butch, and bring women to their knees because she's so hot. I love it. And I found my way to be in the world."

She reached out, tilted my chin up till I had to meet her eyes. "My ridiculous love. It's not that you are butch. It's always the toughest butches who are the biggest marshmallows inside. It's that you play a role. You're scared to let out what's inside, so you've found a persona that works for you. I can't get enough of you on stage, don't get me wrong. When I see you pose in all your leathers, swaggering about, I could come just from looking at you. But that's not who I love. I love you, the one inside that armor. She's the one I want to be with. It's not about whether you carry my bags or not, silly, it's about you being yourself, not you acting a certain way because you're playing a role."

She was right. I thought about her words as I lay awake that night, Christine snuggled close against me, her chestnut hair spread out on my chest. I stroked the soft strands, my thoughts swirling like some cheesy TV effect. My Herman act protected me the way my leather armor protected me when I rode my bike. Just the way the cowhide would shred instead of my skin if I ever fell, my tough persona took the scrapes my inner self was protected from. That was all right out in the world, I felt, but not here, not in my bed with the woman I love. She was the alpha female in this pack, and if I wanted to keep her, I had to flop over, expose my tender throat to her, and show my trust in her by my vulnerability. If I could. The thought made my breath catch in my throat with fear. Still, for Christine, I'd try anything.

Letting her hair stream through my fingers, I reflected on my behavior toward her. I realized that I'd sometimes treated her in ways I would never have put up with. Christine, more of a philosopher than I, simply laughed at me. Like the time I insisted on taking the hammer away from her and then spent an hour cursing and sloppily assembling the shelves she'd been constructing with grace and ease. The shelves she fixed as soon as I left the apartment. The black leather skirt she wanted me to buy that I'd refused to get, even though I saw how good it looked on me, just because it didn't fit the image I'd constructed. I was being as obnoxious in my way as the pathetic posing boys of my small-town youth, desperate to prove their masculinity through stupid stunts and sexual bragging. My smart woman was right. Butch was one thing, acting like a jerk was quite another.

Not that that changed my behavior any. Unfortunately, one just doesn't let go of habits just because one's realized the neurosis underlying them. I still insisted on grabbing her packages, opening her doors—treating her as fragile, though I knew she was far stronger that I was. I drove her crazy, but she stayed.

At least I hoped that was what she wanted to do. As the days and weeks slipped by, getting closer and closer to our anniversary, I started to see less and less of her. I started to wonder if I needed to put a private detective on her trail. She came home late, exhausted, and wouldn't tell me what was going on, just that it was a secret and I'd find out soon. I was half grateful for her absence; I had a lot of work to finish. I work at home, and when I have a deadline, I start to resemble a bear woken from hibernation by drunken backcountry snowboarders. Still, I couldn't help wondering where she was. I confronted her a few times, and she reminded me that our anniversary was coming up, so I should calm down. Even so, I'm a worrier by nature.

On the day of our anniversary, we both slept in and then had breakfast in bed. Then dessert in bed. We walked on the beach, went for a nice dinner, and went dancing. We swayed together all night, clinging together no matter how fast the song, then, after munching postparty fries at the twenty-four-hour Denny's, we wound up in her dance studio, watching the sun slowly rise and fill the room with light. She slipped away, leaving me sprawled in the corner of the studio. Christine came back, dressed in her tutu, and whispered, "I created a new solo dance for you, my love."

As I sat in the corner of the white room like a lump of coal on a snowbank, watching the early morning light bathe her in a shell-pink glow, all the doubts of the past few weeks slipped away. I would have felt awful about mistrusting her if I wasn't so happy, but the self-recrimination could, and no doubt would, come tomorrow. I could feel my love for her swell in my chest, threatening to break me apart, tear me down.

The music reached the notes she needed, and she began to dance. She wore the traditional ballerina drag: pink leotard and gauzy pink skirt. She rose on her toes, began to swirl about. Her moves were delicate, fragile, graceful. She was the epitome of femininity as she leaped and swirled. I looked hungrily at the curve of her arm, the lines of her leg, the shape of her breast. She looked like a figurine. My arms ached to enfold her. Trace out the curves of her with my hands, my lips, my tongue.

But then, somehow, her movements changed. They became those of the figurine I was comparing her to. I gasped as I realized how completely she knew me. Her dance became a parody of womanhood, an excess of femininity, faintly ridiculous. I had no idea how she did it, because she was still making the same leaps and twirls, but somehow her dance had become satire. She mimed feminine rituals, makeup, frilly clothes—high-femme style made ludicrous through her magnificent talent. I could see how hampering the weight of girlish ritual was, a constriction into a simpering, prancing role. Suddenly, she collapsed gracefully, fainting dead away, falling into a set of imaginary arms I practically saw, so perfect were her movements. And then her dance changed. Her skirt fell away, she swirled around somehow, and she became the sturdy butch into whose arms she'd fallen.

As the music slid into a throbbing, masculine beat, her whole demeanor changed. She drew out a black tie from her bodice and wrapped it around her neck, turning into a guy with just that simple prop. Her moves had all the swaggering grace I'd ever longed for. As she posed and strutted, I realized that she was dancing my act, the one I'd done when I'd first met her. Except she was doing as it should be done, as a dancer would do it, posing and flowing from movement to movement, with an attitude I'd never even hoped to attain.

I grew hopelessly wet as I watched her confident, sexual poses, felt the clutch of her fingers on my own groin when she grabbed her crotch, felt the tingling shock of a tweaked nipple as she brushed her hand across her chest. Then, as they had before, her movements became satire, mocking masculine pretensions. She moved her shoulders back and forth, clutched her crotch, and her movements brought into high relief the absurdity of it, the inanity of clutching after a hunk of flesh (or in my case, silicone) to prove an identity.

The music changed again, became a laughing, joyous song, as her movements changed with it. She discarded the choking black tie and ripped off her leotard with an ecstatic gesture of release, of freedom, of joy. She twirled, naked, sexless, purely human, purely herself, leaping across the floor with the gestures of childhood, an imaginary childhood where nothing mattered but the warm yellow sun and the laughter of friends and the joy of movement. As she twirled, I could feel the droplets of joy spray out from her fingertips the way water sprays from a sprinkler. I soaked up her love like a parched lawn.

She reached down and grabbed me, and I joined her dance, holding her hands and running around and around and around in a circle. I grabbed her, swept her up in my arms, pressing her against my chest, and twirled her up and down the length of the studio until I had to set her down or drop her. When my head stopped spinning, I found my clothing gone, my woman running her fingertips down my arms. I drank in the sight of her, her slight breasts, the tips hard and rosy, her slim hips, high, firm ass, and incredible legs. She slid away from me, dancing a dance of seduction, running her hands down her body, swaying her hips, extending her leg out to the side so I could see her red, wet cunt under its wild tangle of chestnut curls. I swallowed, dry mouthed, and felt a bead of wetness escape my cunt and roll down my inner thigh. I had never wanted her so much.

She twirled back to me, and I grabbed her. I sank down, pausing at her nipples, nipping at them, sucking them, holding her against me as if I could suck her essence into me through those rosy nipples. I slid to my knees, tracing my tongue down her stomach, dipping it into her belly button, twirling my tongue around it, in and out of it, giving her a teasing foretaste of what I would do between her legs. I slid down farther, my hands cupping her ass, my fingers dipping down between her legs. I dropped my head to her cunt, my tongue parting the dripping curls, feeling the hairs catch in my teeth, drinking in her juices, desperately licking, and sucking and tasting.

I knelt before her, worshipping her, putting all my love into the way I touched her, thanking her for the lesson she had taught me. Oh, I'd still swagger and carry her bags, and she'd still dress in a miniskirt and walk all over me with her pointed heels, but I'd seen beneath all that, seen her heart, seen how deeply she understood me, and now I knew I could show her my heart.

I held her tight within the circle of my arms, drinking her down, and I felt her, moaning, clutching my hair, dragging her nails over my shoulders, crying out. My world shrank to the red-black darkness behind my eyelids, to the musky smell of her, the salty taste, the feel of her springy hair and slick, smooth cunt under my tongue. I ceased to feel even the clamoring of my own body as I focused everything I had on her.

She pulled me away from her cunt and I moaned with loss. Christine slipped out of my arms and sank to the floor beside me. She pushed me down on my side and lay beside me, her head in front of my cunt, her cunt in front of me. I grabbed for her, desperate to taste her again, and felt her tongue deep in me at the same time. I gasped, shuddered at the feeling, then bent my head to her cunt. We merged, then, became one. Our tongues moved at the same speed, our fingers moved to the same spots, we shuddered and moaned in tandem. I felt my orgasm approaching, a great electrical rush that came closer and closer, spreading tingling energy through my limbs. I felt Christine's muscles clenching under me, knew she was as close as I, and then we came, together, our backs arching, our cries muffled by the other's cunt. I was flooded with feeling, my clit burning, my nipples throbbing, sparks shooting down my arms and legs.

I sank back, exhausted, onto the pillow of her thigh. When I opened my eyes, with difficulty, I saw our reflections in the mirrors that surrounded us. We were coiled together, heads resting on thighs, legs curled in, fetal. We made a yin-yang sign together, twined around each other. Black and white, male and female. Light and dark. Except there was no black and white this time, no light and dark, no male and female. Just two humans together, drawn in flesh tones, mellow, graceful, blending gently into one another. We were different, true, but we were not opposites. We lay together side by side, easily fitting into each other's hollows. Christine sighed and raised her head. I gazed at her over our entwined bodies and looked deep into her eyes. "Thank you," I whispered to her and, unable to help myself, I raised her hand to my lips and gently kissed it.

I guess some things never change.

ABOUT THE AUTHORS

STEPHEN ALBROW is a full-time porn writer from England. He is a regular contributor to *She-Male International,* as well as the author of two transvestite novellas, *Adam or Eve?* and *King of Queens,* both published by www.magsinc.com.

HELEN BOYD is the author of *My Husband Betty,* which was a finalist for a Lambda Literary Award, and the follow-up memoir, *She's Not the Man I Married* (Seal Press). She writes about gender and trans issues for her blog *(en)gender,* which can be found online at www.myhusbandbetty.com. She lives with her partner, Betty, in Brooklyn, New York.

TULSA BROWN is an escaped novelist who's been having a good time in erotica since 2004. Her short stories have appeared in well over a dozen anthologies, including *Stirring Up a Storm, Wet Nightmares, Wet Dreams, Glamour Girls,* and the Erotica Readers and Writers Association anthology, *Cream.* She was a runner-up for the Rauxa Prize for Erotic Literature in 2006 and 2007. She is ruined for any sort of real job.

ANDREA DALE misses the casual androgyny and the music of the eighties. She is the author of two novels published by Virgin Books. Her website is at www.cyvarwydd.com

RYAN FIELD is a thirty-year-old freelance writer who lives and works in both Bucks County, PA, and Los Angeles, CA, with his partner of fifteen years and a red poodle. In the last ten years, his fiction has appeared in anthologies and collections; the most recent is *Ultimate Gay Erotica 2007*. He also contributes interviews with celebrities and web masters to www.bestgayblogs. com. He's currently working on a novel.

T. HITMAN is the glammed-up, well-manicured nom de porn of a full-time professional writer who has penned multitudes of short stories, novels, and feature articles, along with a few nonfiction books and the occasional teleplay. His dressed-down alter ego lives with his long-time husband and their adopted rescue cat in a very small writer's bungalow set among the pines on a large plot of forested woods. Most of the time, he pads around the little house barefoot in shorts and old T-shirts, sans heels and mascara. Most of the time.

DEBRA HYDE narrowly avoided being name Priscilla, a fact that still raises the hackles of her tomboy inner child. She grew up running around outside, hunting frogs and salamanders—definitely more a "puppy dog tails" than "sugar and spice and everything nice" kind of kid. Her erotic fiction has been widely anthologized and her first novel, *Inequities,* was published in England in 2007. Visit her at her long-running weblog, Pursed Lips (pursedlips.com).

MELINDA JOHNSTON is a writer from Vancouver, BC, who has been published in *The Perfect Valentine, The Good Parts, Hot & Bothered 4, Outlooks,* and *Xtra West.* You might also catch her on stage doing a little drag.

STAN KENT is a chameleon-hair-colored, former nightclub-owning, rocket scientist author of erotic novels who grew up in England and has a firsthand knowledge of the punishment handed out by sexy schoolteachers. Stan has penned nine original, unique, and very naughty works, including the *Shoe Leather* series. Selections from his books have been featured in the *Best of Erotic Writing* collections. Stan has hosted an erotic talk show night at Hustler Hollywood for the last five years. *The Los Angeles Times* described his monthly performances as "combination moderator and lion tamer." Visit Stan at www.StanKent.com or email him at stan@stankent.com.

ANDREA MILLER is the associate editor at the international Buddhist magazine *The Shambhala Sun* and is doing her MFA in creative writing part time through the University of British Columbia. Her erotica has been published in a variety of print anthologies, including *Best Women's Erotica 2005, Lessons in Love,* and *Travelrotica,* and it has been published on various Internet sites, including Good Vibes and Ruthie's Club.

ELSPETH POTTER lives in Philadelphia. Her stories have appeared in *Best Lesbian Erotica, Best Women's Erotica, Tough Girls, The Mammoth Book of Best New Erotica, Fishnet Magazine, The MILF Anthology,* and *Sex in the System: Stories of Erotic Futures, Technological Stimulation,* and *The Sensual Life of Machines.* Her most recent story, "The Token," appeared in Meredith Schwartz's e-anthology *Alleys and Doorways* in December 2006.

TERESA NOELLE ROBERTS writes erotica, poetry, romance, and speculative fiction. Her erotica has appeared in *Best Women's Erotica 2004, 2005,* and *2007, Secret Slaves: Erotic Stories of Bondage, Caught Looking: Erotic Tales of Voyeurs and Exhibitionists, He's on Top, She's on Top,* and many other publications. She is also one-half of the erotica-writing duo Sophie Mouette, whose novel *Cat Scratch Fever* was released in 2006 by Black Lace Books. She's an unrepentant clotheshorse with a yen for silk and cashmere.

JASON RUBIS lives in Washington, DC. His fiction has appeared in many anthologies, including *Secret Slaves, Sexiest Soles, Leather, Lace and Lust, Garden of Perverse,* and *Blood Surrender.*

LISABET SARAI has been writing ever since she learned how to hold a pencil. She is the author of three erotic novels, *Raw Silk, Incognito,* and *Ruby's Rules,* and two short-story collections, *Fire* and *Rough Caress.* She also edited the ground-breaking anthology *Sacred Exchange,* which explores the spiritual aspects of BDSM relationships, and *Cream: The Best of the Erotica Readers and Writers Association.* Lisabet also works as a freelance editor, reviews books and films for the Erotica Readers and Writers Association (www.erotica-readers.com) and Sliptongue. com, and is a Celebrity Author at Custom Erotica Source (www. customeroticasource.com). Visit her website, Lisabet Sarai's Fantasy Factory (ww.lisabetsarai.com), for more information and samples of her writing.

MARCY SHEINER has written and/or edited over a dozen books. Her fiction, essays, and poetry have been widely anthologized, most recently in *My Body of Knowledge,* edited by

Karen Myers and Felicia Ferlin (Pagefree Publishing 2006). Her
rants, raves, and a bit of erotic fiction can be read on her blog:
marcys.wordpress.com.

Called by *San Francisco* magazine "our erotica king," **SIMON
SHEPPARD** is the editor of *Homosex: Sixty Years of Gay Erotica* and the author of *In Deep: Erotic Stories, Kinkorama: Dis-
patches from the Front Lines of Perversion, Sex Parties 101,*
and the award-winning *Hotter Than Hell and Other Stories.*
His work also appears in well over 200 anthologies, including
many editions of *Best American Erotica* and *Best Gay Erotica.*
He writes the syndicated column "Sex Talk," and hangs out at
www.simonsheppard.com. It's been many years since he put on
a dress.

Called "a trollop with a laptop" by *East Bay Express,* **ALISON
TYLER** is naughty and she knows it. Ms. Tyler is the author of
more than twenty explicit novels, including *Learning to Love It,
Strictly Confidential, Sweet Thing, Sticky Fingers,* and *Something
About Workmen* (all published by Black Lace), and *Rumors* and
Tiffany Twisted (Cheek). Her novels and short stories have been
translated into Japanese, Dutch, German, Italian, Norwegian,
and Spanish. Her stories have appeared in anthologies including
Sweet Life I & II, Taboo, Best Women's Erotica 2002, 2003,
and *2005, Best of Best Women's Erotica, Best Fetish Erotica,*
and *Best Lesbian Erotica 1996* (all published by Cleis); and in
Wicked Words 4, 5, 6, 8 and *10, Sex in the Office, Sex on Holiday,* and *Sex in Uniform* (all published by Black Lace). She is
the editor of *Heat Wave, Best Bondage Erotica, Volumes 1* and
*2, The Merry XXXMas Book of Erotica, Luscious, Exposed,
Happy Birthday Erotica,* and *Three-Way,* and the co-editor of
Caught Looking with Rachel Kramer Bussel (all from Cleis

Press); and the *Naughty Stories from A to Z* series, the *Down &
Dirty* series, *Naked Erotica,* and *Juicy Erotica* (all from Pretty
Things Press). Please visit www.prettythingspress.com.

VERONICA VERA (missvera.com) is the author of *Miss Vera's
Finishing School for Boys Who Want to Be Girls: Tips, Tales
and Teachings from the Dean of the World's First Crossdressing
Academy* (Doubleday) and *Miss Vera's Crossdress for Success: A
Resource Guide for Boys Who Want to Be Girls* (Villard). Miss
Vera's Academy is in New York City. Brochure and application
upon request.

ABOUT THE EDITOR

RACHEL KRAMER BUSSEL is a prolific erotica writer, editor, journalist, and blogger. She serves as senior editor at *Penthouse Variations*, hosts the In the Flesh Erotic Reading Series, and wrote the popular "Lusty Lady" column for *The Village Voice*. Her books include *Naughty Spanking Stories from A to Z 1* and *2, First-Timers, Up All Night, Glamour-Girls: Femme/Femme Erotica, Ultimate Undies, Sexiest Soles, Secret Slaves: Erotic Stories of Bondage, Sex and Candy: Sugar Erotica, Caught Looking: Erotic Tales of Voyeurs and Exhibitionism, Hide and Seek, Best Sex Writing 2008,* and the kinky companion volumes *He's on Top: Erotic Stories of Male Dominance and Female Submission* and *She's on Top: Erotic Stories of Female Dominance and Male Dominance.* Her twin odes to bottoming, *Yes, Sir: Erotic Stories of Female Submission and Male Dominance* and *Yes, Ma'am: Erotic Stories of Male Submission and Female Dominance,* will be published by Cleis Press in February 2008, and her first novel, *Everything But...,* will be published by Bantam in summer 2008.

Her writing has been published in over 100 anthologies, including *Best American Erotica 2004* and *2006*, as well as *AVN*, *Bust*, Cleansheets.com, Cosmo UK, *Diva*, *Girlfriends*, Huffington Post, Mediabistro.com, *New York Post*, Oxygen.com, *Penthouse*, *Playgirl*, *Punk Planet*, *San Francisco Chronicle*, *Time Out New York*, and *Zink*. In her spare time, she hunts down the country's best cupcakes and blogs about them at cupcakestakethecake.blogspot.com. Visit her at www.rachelkramerbussel.com.